Jordan ran his tongue against the sensitive ridges at the top of her mouth, before he withdrew it.

"Oh," she whimpered. "Ooh. Ooh. Wonderful."

"We can't do this." Jordan groaned and turned his face to the side. "Not with Trevor right here."

She levered herself up on her elbows again. "Can't do what? Obviously we can do this. We just did."

"You know what I mean."

The moment had passed, more surely than if he'd dumped a bucket of cold water over her. She rolled off him, onto her back beside him, desperate to regain her dignity. "Yes, I know what you mean. And no, we can't do it. I never intended to. It's not in the contract."

"Then why—"

She shrugged and lied through her teeth. "Why not? It was fun." *Remember to keep your tone light, Rosemary. Regain the initiative. Don't tell the man that every time he touches you, you feel as if you've been eating prairie locoweed.*

She ran the palm of her hand across his face. "You need to enjoy life, Jordan Sterling. To remember you're young and good-looking and desirable."

He breathed deeply and threw his arm up to shade his eyes. "I have to work a ranch. I can't be a playboy."

She tickled the tip of his nose with a piece of grass as earlier he had tickled hers. "So, how many cows died this afternoon while you flirted with me?"

He nodded with a rueful smile. "You're some woman, Rosemary Robbins. My Rose. In fact, I wish—"

He broke off when Trevor whimpered.

A wave of regret washed over Rosemary. What would Jordan have told her, or asked her? It might have been most interesting.

It might have changed her life.

The Rancher's Rose

by

Wilma Fasano

The Rancher's Rose

COPYRIGHT © 2007 by Wilma Fasano

Cover Art by *Tamra Westberry*

The Wild Rose Press
PO Box 706
Adams Basin, NY 14410-0706
Visit us at www.thewildrosepress.com

Publishing History
First Yellow Rose Edition, 2007
Print ISBN 1-60154-105-8

Published in the United States of America

Dedication

To my wonderful friends and critique partners Lynn, Lee, and Loretta. To my editors, Rhonda Penders and Spencer Glenn.

Chapter One

Rosemary Robbins peered through the windshield into the worsening storm.

Two days ago she'd fled Winnipeg in the middle of the night, bolting with baby Trevor, desperately searching for safety. Early this morning, she'd driven west from Calgary on rural roads, following the signs to the small town she sought. Then the storm began. Somewhere Rosemary had taken a wrong turn and now had no idea where she was. She knew only that the storm mushroomed in ferocity while the road narrowed and became increasingly impassable.

Her small car slued sideways, and she braked, trying to maintain control. Slowly but inexorably, the car slid across the shoulder of the road and into the ditch.

After turning to check on Trevor in the backseat, Rosemary punched in 911 on her cell phone, but received a *no signal* message. Surprise. Between the surrounding hills and the thickening snow, a cell phone signal would have been a miracle.

Could she walk to find help? Carrying Trevor? She wasn't sure she had any other option.

She stepped out of the car and sank up to her ankles in snow. Each time she tried to take a step, she slithered on the treacherous icy surface that lurked underfoot. All she could see was an endless sea of white on the ground and in the air.

Rosemary had no choice but to wait and hope for rescue. Before getting back in, she opened the back door to double check on Trevor. Miraculously he still slept. A blanket lay beside him on the seat and she pulled it up over both him and the teddy bear he clutched in his arms, tucking it in firmly to conserve heat. Love surged through her, and she was careful not to waken the child. He was better off, they were both better off, if he continued to sleep.

She loved Trevor desperately, but had she made the right decision? Had she rescued him from her sister Blair, only to have him perish in this storm? She snicked the back door closed quietly and crept back into the driver's seat.

Once there, she turned the radio on low and listened through the static to the information that the storm was expected to worsen, that temperatures would fall throughout the day, that snow plows would not reach rural roads for several days.

"Oh, great!" Rosemary turned off the ignition to save the battery and fuel. She might need the heater even more later on.

She settled back in the seat, hoping against hope that someone would find her. Preferably the driver of a tow truck.

Wait! What was that?

A dark shape loomed up in the middle of the road in front of her. She sat up straight and peered through the windshield, squinting through the slanting snow, trying to see more clearly. The white flakes, fat and damp as soapsuds, splattered against the glass.

When she exhaled, her breath left a patch of steam on the windshield, and she wiped away the condensation with the back of her hand. Was that a bear or a moose? It sure wasn't a tow truck.

Gradually a shadowy figure on a black horse emerged from the clusters of snow flakes, finally resolving into the form of a cowboy, complete with a black Stetson, heavy jacket, and chaps. A frisson of fear swept through Rosemary.

She was being paranoid. Of course, she was. This man had nothing to do with Blair and her new husband, could not possibly be part of the plot to kidnap and sell Trevor. In spite of the attempt to reassure herself, she still clutched the steering wheel so tightly her nails bit into her palms. Then she took a deep breath and consciously unclenched her fingers.

Earlier that morning, back in Calgary, before she drove into this terrible storm, the sun shone and the bright sky gleamed cornflower blue. A young man at a filling station said that some folks would pay a lot for a cute baby like Trevor. It was just idle conversation, a friendly remark intended to be a compliment. But just the same, the comment had sent splinters of fear through her, both at the time and now in her remembering of it.

She rotated her shoulders, trying to relax and shake off her fears. *The real danger is the storm*, she repeated to herself several times.

The man maneuvered his horse until it sidled up to the car, then leaned over till he was nose-to-nose with Rosemary and rapped on the window. No more than three inches and a thin piece of glass separated their faces. Snow weighted the brim of his black Stetson so it sloped down, hiding his upper face. A red bandana tied over his nose and mouth obscured everything else but his intense blue eyes, and the straight line of his black brows that came within a half-inch of meeting above his nose.

She made a megaphone of her hands and yelled at Black Hat through the glass. "Please go somewhere and phone for a tow truck."

Instead, the rider dismounted, then shook his head and gestured for her to unlock the car. The horse positioned its rump to the wind and stood only a few feet from the car, with its head hanging down. Flecks of water formed on the saddle where fallen snowflakes melted from the man's recent warmth.

She tried again. "Please. Just call a tow truck for us."

The man pounded on the glass. "You can't stay in there. You'll freeze to death waiting for a tow truck in this storm." He peered at the back seat. "I won't hurt you, I promise. I'll get you to safety."

Rosemary had to believe him. Already, she felt the cold, and it was still the middle of the morning. What would happen when night came? Just the same, she wished he'd have called a tow truck. She glanced over her right shoulder. Trevor still slept undisturbed in his car seat. Sitting here until she froze to death wouldn't help the baby. She gritted her teeth and forced herself to pull up the lock.

The man jerked the car door open and then stopped moving to stare slack-jawed at her shorts and bare legs.

Rosemary bristled at the implied censure. "It was in the eighties when I left Winni—uh, when I left home. I've got more clothes in the trunk."

He nodded, gave her a hint of a smile. "It was in the eighties here yesterday, too. This is a very unpredictable climate. Do you have a coat?"

She shook her head. "It's the middle of May. All I have is a sweater and a light jacket. And jeans."

"And the baby?"

"About the same. I have blankets."

"O-kay." He dragged the word out.

Rosemary grimaced. She really hadn't been thinking when she'd packed. "I'll get my jeans and jacket from the trunk."

"Let's do it." He nodded and moved the horse back from the door.

Rosemary got out of the car and stood. The snow was now halfway to her knees. She shivered and crossed her arms over her breasts for protection when the gusting wind struck her, and instant goose bumps materialized on her exposed skin. She could hardly tell this stranger that she'd grabbed her computer and an armful of clothes and fled, so instead she suppressed her concerns and opened the back door.

Secure in his car seat, Trevor still slept, his cheek snuggled against the bright red cloak of Little Red Riding Hood, which formed part of the design on the padded upholstery. Only sixteen months old, the baby blew soft bubbles when he exhaled. A lump swelled up in the blanket where his baby arms clutched an already-worn teddy bear that Rosemary had given him for his first birthday. Just looking at him made her heart swell with fierce love and pride.

The cowboy leaned past Rosemary, lifted the blanket aside and undid the straps that secured Trevor, tenderly lifting him out. He tucked one arm under Trevor's legs and supported his head with the other, holding him like a newborn instead of a robust toddler. He carefully protected the stuffed bear in Trevor's arms, then rested the baby's head against his shoulder so he could place the blanket back over him.

Trevor awoke and rubbed his eyes. "Uncah?" he asked. "Uncah?"

Rosemary cringed. Trevor had called all of Blair's

million or so male friends uncle. It had been the first word he'd learned to say. But none of those uncles had ever been as solicitous as this stranger. She felt the first stirrings of hope. Maybe she and Trevor really were safe.

"Come on," the man called. "Get whatever you need for the baby and let's go."

"Oh. Oh, yes. The bag. I need the bag in the back seat. His diapers and things."

She grabbed the bag and handed it to the cowboy, who slung it over the saddle horn. Then she shoved in the locks and slammed the car door.

"All right. Don't you have clothes in the trunk?"

The trunk. The keys. The locked car. Rosemary's face flamed with embarrassment. Twenty-eight years old and so rattled she'd locked the keys in the car. She waved her hands toward the vehicle, pointed at the lock buttons, and shrugged.

"Smart move." The stranger placed Trevor into her arms.

Then he picked her up, complete with Trevor and teddy bear, and hoisted her into the saddle backwards, so that she straddled the horse, facing its tail. She clutched the baby tightly, trusting the man to know what he was doing.

The cowboy took off his sheepskin coat and bundled it around the pair of them. The fleece-lined garment retained the heat from his body, sheltering and warming both her and Trevor, while its owner stood in the storm wearing jeans, leather chaps, and a red flannel shirt.

"But—"

"It's all right." He fastened the coat toggles, binding Rosemary and Trevor together. Then he swung up behind the saddle. "We can't let the little guy get cold."

Something about that tugged at Rosemary's heart strings. Only a good man would take off his coat in a storm to keep a baby warm.

"Lean forward." He motioned her face toward his chest. "So you can rest your head against me, to protect the little guy."

She obeyed, wrapping her arms around Trevor to secure him. Then she leaned forward and rested her cheek against the stranger's chest. His flannel shirt was already damp from the fresh snow. Drops of water from the brim of his Stetson trickled down Rosemary's face, onto her neck, and dribbled under the collar of the sheepskin coat. The heart that beat against her cheek felt strong and steady.

"Sorry about your legs." The man's voice echoed from somewhere above her head. "I'll try to get you to my place before your feet and legs freeze." He clucked and the horse began to move.

The cowboy's chaps banged against Rosemary's bare knees, so she shifted her legs away. "No, keep your legs still. Here. I'll put mine over yours for warmth. It might help a bit."

"All right, I'll try." It wasn't likely that he heard her.

He covered her legs with his, then nudged the horse, goading it into a slow gallop. His arms trapped her, and his legs pinned hers against the wide flaps above the stirrup. The wet leather chafed the undersides of her legs, while the backs of the stranger's chaps irritated the tops of them.

What should she do next? Ask this cowboy if he knew where she could find the Sterling ranch? She'd fled without having a plan firmly in place. Somehow, she'd assumed instinct would show her the next step. She prayed silently for guidance.

She wanted the ride to be over so she could get Trevor somewhere dry and warm. Yet how could any spot be more dry and warm than where the child now snuggled, absorbing the heat of her body, warm in the sheepskin coat, secured by the strong arms of the stranger?

The wind stung the exposed flesh of her legs in the places where neither saddle flaps nor chaps protected them. Wet flakes of snow soaked her sneakers and her short white summer socks. The cold wind turned them chill and stiff. When she was certain she could no longer stand the jolting movement of the horse and the prickling of leather like cold sandpaper against her legs, she heard, "Whoa, Satan."

The horse slowed and stopped. Rosemary lifted her head to look around, but found her eyelids stuck shut. When she stretched them and blinked, they separated far enough for her to see through the frozen snow that still lay heavy as mascara on her lashes. She blinked again with a rapid up-and-down motion, sending tiny shards of ice cascading over the sheepskin coat. The stranger swung off the horse.

Rosemary saw a sprawling log ranch-house that blended into the snow and the shadowy grove of trees behind it.

"Better let me take the little fellow first."

"His name's Trevor."

The stranger stood beside Rosemary. He held his fleece-lined leather gloves in his teeth while he undid the toggles of the coat and lifted Trevor from his warm nest.

"Trevor." He mumbled around the gloves, then put them back on and repeated, "Trevor. You're okay now, little guy." His head swiveled toward Rosemary. "Stay where you are." As if she were capable of doing anything else.

He carried Trevor to the veranda and plunked him on an old-fashioned porch swing, then returned to the horse. Satan stood statue-like with lowered head. Would his owner be equally tractable?

She would soon know, but the way he'd treated Trevor gave her hope. The man lifted her down and handed her the diaper bag he'd slung over the saddle horn. Then he carried her through the snow until he could stand her upright on the dry floorboards of the porch.

Her legs were stiff and lifeless, like in one of those nightmares where you try to run but your legs refuse to move. She looked down and saw they were red from the chafing. The snow she shook from her hair puddled around her feet on the porch.

The stranger yanked his bandana down, then took Trevor from the swing, opened the door, and strode through a slate-floored entry hall with the baby in his arms, leaving Rosemary to trot at his heels as best she could. The sudden heat of the house made her legs prickle with a thousand needles.

A warm bright room at the end of the short hall welcomed them. Cheerful hand-woven area rugs partially covered the wooden floors. A cream-colored leather sofa filled one end of the room. At the other end, two matching recliners sat angled in front of a wood stove, where a few embers glowed behind the glass door.

Rosemary stood in the middle of the floor and studied the cowboy. Between the ice and snow on his upper face and the dark stubble on the lower, his face wasn't much more visible than it had been before. She shifted her weight from one sodden foot to the other. What should her next move be?

"Here." The stranger plucked the sheepskin coat from her back and tossed it onto a chair, then handed Trevor to her, and stuck out his right hand. "Jordan Sterling."

Rosemary felt as if all the blood had drained from her face. Hopefully, Jordan would blame it on the cold. She wasn't ready to deal with this yet, hadn't fully thought out how she would approach the man when she found him.

She took a deep breath and clasped his hand. "Rosemary Robbins." The name didn't appear to mean anything to him.

His handshake was firm and brief. "Afraid I've got to desert you. I've got cattle to take care of."

"I understand," Rosemary assured him. "We'll be fine."

"The bedroom wing's to your left." He gestured as he spoke. "My bedroom's the big one you come to first, and if you go in and turn right, you'll find the bathroom. I'm out of here in five minutes. After that, it's all yours. The Jacuzzi would be a great place for the two of you to warm up."

He paused, then went on. "Look, I'm really sorry about this. I know I'm not showing much hospitality, but the livestock can't wait. Make yourself at home."

Rosemary saw him look at her legs, and followed his glance. They'd turned a mottled mixture of blue and gray.

"The kitchen's that way." He jerked his thumb to indicate the direction. "Once you're warm, go ahead and make yourself something to eat. If you want a nap, you can use my bed. Use the washer and dryer if you need to."

One corner of his mouth turned up in the beginning of a grin. "Sorry my clothes won't fit you very well, but if you can find a shirt or something to cover you while your own clothes dry, you're welcome to it."

He threw a couple of logs on the smoldering embers in the stove. "Keep the fire going, if you want to and know how."

"Yes. I know how. Go ahead and look after your cows. We'll be fine. Thanks for everything." She smiled weakly and tried a joke. "I promise I won't take off with the family silver."

He actually chuckled. "You couldn't get anywhere with it in this weather. I'll turn up the thermostat on my way out."

He wheeled and went into the bedroom wing. A minute later he emerged, wearing a dry flannel shirt—blue, this time, the color of his eyes—and a clean dry bandana around the lower part of his face. He retrieved the sheepskin coat, put it on, and left the house. Rosemary heard the furnace come on, and within a couple minutes the house began to warm up.

In all that time, she hadn't said anything about Trevor, couldn't have. She couldn't trot around the house after him gasping out, *You have a son. You have a son. You have a son.*

Hardly. The big revelation should be made when she had time to announce it and to answer his questions. And not until she'd found out a little more about him, about whether or not he had the resources—or the inclination—to care for a child.

After Rosemary heard the outside door slam behind him, she turned her attention to getting warm. The bathroom was modern and sumptuous, complete with Jacuzzi, shower, large vanity, walk-in closet, and snow-covered skylight. Jordan Sterling appeared to live alone, but he certainly lived in luxury.

She remembered the oil wells she'd seen as she'd driven from Calgary, the pumps looking like giant grasshoppers dipping their heads up and down in the fields and pastures. Maybe Jordan Sterling's income wasn't limited to what he got from selling cows.

After she and Trevor had soaked in a tub full of warm water, Rosemary slipped a clean pair of Jordan's heavy socks on her feet and found a black and red checked flannel shirt that she could drape around her naked body. The scent of Jordan Sterling's heavy shirt hinted of horses, leather, and after-shave. It made her think of the owner—strong, masculine and, she hoped, reliable.

She laid Trevor on the vanity and diapered him. For the moment, she forgot about the bizarre situation in the rush of love she felt for Trevor.

"Piggies." Trevor lay on his back, hands and feet churning in the air like miniature windmills. "Piggies. Piggies."

Rosemary rubbed her nose against his stomach, and breathed in the wonderful scents of clean baby and talcum powder. Then she ran her finger across the crease that separated his toes from the sole of his foot. His toes were soft and rosy, warm from the bath, each perfect little toe topped by a shell-pink perfect little nail.

He kicked his feet as if doing a bicycling exercise. "Piggies." He crowed and chortled. "Piggies."

"Okay," she agreed. "Piggies. This little pig went to market." She shook his big toe. "This little pig stayed home." She jiggled the next one.

Trevor squealed with delight, and chanted, "Piggies. Piggies. Mawket. Home."

"This little pig had roast beef." The third toe. "This little pig had none."

After number four, she improvised. The words for the fifth toe varied every time they played the game. "This little pig rode a big black horse." She bunched her fingers, and moved them over Trevor's tummy, imitating the four hooves of a galloping horse, then tickled toe number five.

Then she reverted to the original words of the nursery rhyme as she wiggled the last toe vigorously, "And this little pig cried 'wee, wee, wee,' all the way home."

For on each pink and perfect baby foot, Trevor had six toes.

Rosemary wrapped him in a clean towel and looked into his warm brown eyes. His dark hair curled, wet and rumpled. His rosy face was flushed from the warm water. How could anyone not love such a perfect, cheerful and sunny child? How could his very own mother possibly think of him as only a product for sale to the highest bidder?

Rosemary picked him up and held him close, while

Trevor yawned and beat his hands against her. When she bent her head forward, a loose strand of hair must have tickled him. He grabbed the hair and yanked on it until she yelped. She gently pried his fingers loose and tossed the lock of hair back over her shoulder. Trevor giggled a loud baby giggle.

"Naptime for you, chum." Rosemary carried him out to Jordan's bedroom and tucked him into bed, under a bright patchwork quilt.

After she started their clothes washing, she threw more wood into the stove to keep the blazing flames going. Nothing would take the chill from her body and her heart faster than the comfort of a crackling fire.

She made herself a cup of tea and sat with it in one of the soft leather recliners beside the fire and gazed out the window, which overlooked a patio, a lawn, and a grove of birch trees, now bowed down from heavy snow. The fat white flakes continued to fall. *Mother Goose shaking her feather bed,* her mother used to say of snow like this. Rosemary stared at it, mesmerized, and reflected.

So here was Jordan Sterling, the man she'd driven across the prairies to find. Blair had given her the impression that he lived in a rural shack. Yes, the house had an exterior of weather-beaten logs, but the interior was downright luxurious. The man appeared to live by himself. The house, although tidy and well-kept, lacked the homey atmosphere of a woman's touch. Rosemary drew a forefinger across the end table beside the leather chair, writing her name in the patina of dust. The light coating of dust on everything, the lack of pictures or little knick-knacks—the touches that made a house into a home—all were missing. If she breathed deeply, she could smell the slight musty scent of places where nobody lived.

She swirled the tea in the mug and listened to the chug-slosh, chug-slosh of the washer. How had fate, in this blizzard, led her to the very ranch she'd sought? Had fate been responsible for her rescue by the very man she'd come from Winnipeg to find? The one person who might keep Trevor safe.

Maybe the storm had been a blessing. Now she had an excuse to be here—and a chance to size up Jordan Sterling. She could tell him about Trevor as soon as she decided whether he'd be a fit parent. The storm would give her some of the time she needed for that.

****

Jordan Sterling rode his horse through dripping tree branches and wet snow searching for cattle, especially for cows with young calves. Grown cattle would weather this harsh spring storm nicely, but young calves could die.

He'd left Satan in the barn to rest and saddled Ranger, a big bay with Clydesdale somewhere in his ancestry—heavy enough to plow his way through the snow, carrying, if necessary, a calf slung across the front of the saddle.

Jordan thought of the woman and child he'd rescued from the storm. What were they doing here? She said she'd come from Winnipeg, and her car had a Manitoba license plate. Manitoba was two provinces over. This was a ranching area, not tourist country. If they were looking for a particular ranch, wouldn't she have asked about it? Though he knew he hadn't given her much chance.

When he looked at the woman with her long light hair and calm gray eyes, he remembered things about men and women he'd vowed to forget.

He snorted as he kicked Ranger and plunged down the steep side of the next ravine. The only trustworthy woman he'd ever met had been his mother.

And the little guy? Jordan visualized the child as he'd first seen him, sleeping through the storm, clutching his teddy bear and blowing bubbles. He'd always wanted a child of his own, and seeing Trevor made him feel his loss more bitterly.

The joy of being a father would never be his. He'd known that ever since his ex-wife, in the first year of their marriage, had told him she was sterile.

****

The fire crackled and blazed, the base of the flames blue, the upper parts red and orange and yellow. Rosemary adjusted the draft so the fire would burn less brightly, but with a warm and steady heat. Watching the fire mesmerized her, made her drowsy, and filled her with the memories of the past. Her parents, in the small town north of Winnipeg where she'd been born, had a fireplace in the living room. Rosemary associated it with warmth and love and security, with the sort of life she wanted for Trevor.

Her thoughts rambled on. Would Jordan Sterling provide a life of warmth and love and security, or would he be a parent like Blair? They must have had something in common when he married her. How could a man with the poor judgment to marry Blair show the sort of care for a child that Jordan had already shown for Trevor? But even if he wanted to be a tender and loving father, could this busy rancher, by himself, create a safe and contented life for a child?

She yawned. Right now, she was far too tired to think through all these things. She had made lunch, finished the laundry, given Trevor his evening meal and put him back to bed. She'd also, after hemming and hawing about what she shouldn't do in someone else's house, taken steaks from the freezer for Jordan's supper. Her eyes drifted shut.

Rosemary often knew even in the midst of dreams that she was dreaming. But it didn't seem to matter. The images and the stories they told rolled on. In her dream, she was Trevor's mother. Not his mother's sister, but his actual mother. In her dream, she searched for her child's father. A social worker type of woman led her down rows of men who stood in a line-up like the ones viewed by witnesses to a crime. But in the dream, Rosemary wasn't looking for perps. She was looking for a father for her child. The first man in the line was to die for, but he was blond. He couldn't be Trevor's father. Trevor had brown hair and eyes.

The next man was cute, but he had red hair and freckles. Rosemary shook her head. No, he wasn't the one.

Next were a hundred men in a double line, the men that Blair had referred to as Trevor's uncles. She didn't look long at any of them, but instead marched down the lines, snapping her head to the left and saying, "Not him." No, not him. Never him. Her head swiveled to the right. "Not him." To the left. To the right. No hesitation on any. None of the uncles were good enough to be Trevor's father.

The next man was one of Rosemary's clients, both good-looking and nice. But married. Sadly, she shook her head. No. Not him.

13

The last man in line was a cowboy, a cowboy with a black Stetson and sapphire eyes. She opened her mouth, but before she could speak, her sister Blair marched up the line of men and dragged the cowboy from under Rosemary's nose.

Chapter Two

The sound of the door woke Rosemary. Jordan strode past her, through the family room and to the bedroom wing. He might have caught her napping, but she was determined to be wide awake when he returned. The fire, which had burned low while she slept, would be crackling and cheerful by time he'd changed his clothes. She stood up and put more kindling on, and a couple pieces of wood, then opened the draft. The fire licked at the wood, leaping into flames of red and orange and yellow.

Rosemary sat down again, with her legs tucked under her, and waited. When Jordan returned, his shirt and jeans were clean and his face freshly shaved. He made straight for the fire and slumped into his recliner. Steam rose from his heavy woolen socks.

"I see you put the little guy in my bed?"

"Yes." Rosemary searched his face for signs of displeasure. "You told me to. I'll move him if you tell me where."

"Never mind. I'll bunk in the guest room for now."

Rosemary glanced at her watch. Nine o'clock.

"My going in and out won't bother him?" Jordan asked.

"No. Once he's down, he'd sleep through an earthquake. Unless his teeth disturb him, and then he'd wake up anyway."

Jordan yawned, then glanced at Rosemary. "Nice, uh, outfit you have on."

She still wore his flannel shirt over her freshly washed underclothes. She found it warm and cozy, even more so once she'd taken the belt from her shorts to cinch it around her waist. The shirt came almost to her knees.

Rosemary flushed. "I hope you don't mind. I put this on while my own clothes washed and dried. You told me to find something if I could. And then it was so comfortable, I just left it."

"Sure looks warmer than what you arrived in."

He sat a moment, watching her, then got up, and put more wood in the stove. When he returned, he sat down, raised the footrest and sprawled back in the chair.

Was he asleep?

Rosemary spent the time giving him the once-over, this man she'd crossed parts of three provinces to find. It was a surprisingly pleasant occupation, considering her preconceived ideas.

Hmmm. Good-looking. Downright handsome, in fact. His dark wavy hair was rumpled from being crushed under his hat. Wet strands of it were plastered to his forehead. Eyelashes any woman would kill for fanned against his tanned skin. His face, lean and hard like the rest of him, sported an aristocratic nose. She smiled to herself. *Aristocratic* sounded better than *hooked*. Besides, it wasn't really hooked—just enough to give him a rakish look, a combination of Julius Caesar and Rhett Butler.

She knew from Blair that he was thirty, but now repose smoothed the harsh lines that bracketed his mouth, and he looked boyish and vulnerable. She shook her head. He wasn't a boy. He was a man, a hard-working one, and probably a hungry one. She'd better do something about feeding him. But if she moved, she might wake him. Instead she gazed into the flames through the glass front of the woodstove, and thought about Trevor. She'd come here to rate Jordan Sterling, not for his looks, but as a protector for Trevor.

Finally Jordan stirred and sat up. He stretched. "Guess I'd better rustle up some grub. You eaten yet?"

Rosemary bolted to her feet. "Just Trevor. Not me. I mean, just lunch."

Jordan levered himself from the chair.

Rosemary held out her arm, palm forward. "You sit down. I'll get dinner. I thawed some steaks. I hope you don't mind."

"If I sit down, I'll just fall asleep again. And after I eat, I've got to get back to work."

"You can't work all the time."

"Try telling a day-old calf that." He followed her to the kitchen. "You don't have to get my meal. Honest. You must be worn out after everything you went through this morning."

"I want to." She walked to the steaks and poked one of them to check how much they'd thawed. "I want to do something to pay you back for rescuing us."

"Thanks," he said. "I guess I'd really appreciate it at that. I'm so tired I'm running on empty."

She smiled at him, and the smile froze. He was studying her face as if he were trying to place her. Did Blair have a picture of her that he'd seen? "I'm from Winnipeg," she said, mainly for something to say.

He raised his eyebrows. "Yeah? You started to say that. And I noticed the Manitoba plates on your car. What brings you out here? Looking for any place special? Anybody you need to phone to tell them you're still in one piece?"

"I live alone, and I haven't been gone long enough to alarm anyone." She ignored the first part of his question.

"All right, but you're welcome to use the phone." He pointed to the white phone on the kitchen counter, then glanced toward the sink. He yawned. "Yeah, if you have those steaks defrosted and want to broil them that would be great. There are canned goods in the pantry by the fridge. Maybe I do need a few more minutes rest."

"Why don't you go back and sit down? I'll let you know when it's ready." She turned away, back to the kitchen counter, as he left.

She got the steaks ready to broil and spread frozen French fries on a cookie sheet to pop into the oven. After she had both steak and potatoes cooking, she opened the pantry and looked over the assortment of canned vegetables, then took out a can of green beans while she reflected.

He'd looked at her as if he should know her, but, brother-in-law though he was, she'd had no idea what he looked like. Blair had no pictures of him—not wedding, not casual. Nothing. Almost as if he'd meant nothing at all to her. This man who should be part of Rosemary's family was a total stranger, someone she'd never met once in the three years Blair was married to him.

The smell of sizzling steaks made her mouth water and her stomach growl. She opened the can of beans to heat, walked to the door of the family room and called out,

"Almost ready."

He lounged in the doorway for a moment before coming into the kitchen, still looking at her as if he were trying to place her. His eyes inventoried her, scrutinized her, going over her from the top of her head to his heavy woolen socks which she wore as slippers.

As if he sensed her nervousness and wanted to reassure her that he was harmless, he turned away, facing the wall. "Your little guy's sure cute. I'd give anything to have a baby like that."

Rosemary paused and thought a little prayer. Was this her chance to tell him the truth? Eventually she had to trust someone. She'd driven more than eight hundred miles because Jordan Sterling seemed the best bet.

She stepped back, holding her hands behind her, clinging with them to the edge of the kitchen counter, and crossing her legs at the ankles. She opened her mouth hoping the right words would come out, but he spoke first.

"I appreciate the meal." He plunked himself down at the kitchen table. "But I need to hurry up and get back to work."

She closed her mouth. It was too soon to tell him. She couldn't spring major news like this on him when he had to leave as soon as he could bolt his food. Besides, she still knew very little about him. There was no hurry about telling him, she reminded herself. From the brief radio report she'd heard that morning, she'd have at least three or four days, if not more, before she'd be expected to leave.

****

The next morning, Rosemary looked out on a white world—trees, ground, and sky. The wind still blew and the snow swirled in dizzying patterns.

As she stirred the oatmeal, her mind turned again to Jordan Sterling. What should she tell him about herself and Trevor? How could she get more information about his suitability as a father? Maybe she'd throw out a few casual questions—just in the way of conversation. See if he had any family in the area. Close neighbors. Whether he'd ever had a housekeeper, especially one that might want to take the job up again. Girlfriends. Maiden aunts.

She'd have to space her questions—just pretend to make polite conversation, like she was trying to find things to talk about. Could she possibly discover if he had plans to remarry? He was still a young man. Her heart rebelled against the idea, but her practical mind told her remarriage might make him a better father.

The oatmeal began to plop like miniature volcanoes, so Rosemary sighed and turned the burner off.

Conversation revolving around Jordan could very well lead to conversation revolving around her. Like what was she doing in this part of the country anyway. How would she answer that? Tourists? Yeah, right. How many motels and country inns had she driven by in the hour before she slid off the road? Tourists wanting to experience the mountains obviously went somewhere else.

She wouldn't tell Jordan the truth. Not yet. Not until she'd assured herself that he would protect Trevor against Blair, no matter whose baby he was. At least, Trevor and she were safe for now. The snow was over a foot deep and still falling. No one could get out—or in.

****

By the time Jordan returned for dinner, Rosemary had already fed Trevor and put him to bed for the night. She dished up dinner for herself and Jordan, and sat down in the family eating area.

"You work very hard." She broke a roll and buttered it.

"Ranching's hard work."

"Yes, I suppose so."

The conversation lumbered along, like walking hip-deep through swamp water.

"You can't hire someone to help? Cowboys or ranch hands?"

"Why? I don't have anything else to do with my time. During roundups and branding, I hire extra help. I can handle the work myself the rest of the time."

"Do you have any relatives around?" She tried to keep her voice casual, off-hand. "You know, family you visit sometimes. People who would help you out if you were in a tough spot."

"No." He sent her a shrewd glance over the rim of his coffee cup. "Why are you so interested?"

Rosemary shrugged. "Just making conversation." For the moment she'd better drop the subject. They finished the meal in silence.

****

The next evening, for the third one in a row, Jordan sat down to a hot meal he hadn't had to cook. This could be habit-forming. Rosemary placed a bowl of mashed potatoes on the table, then sat down across from him.

"I wish I could help you with some of your work." She served herself from the bowl. "But I don't know anything about ranches, and even if I did, I couldn't leave Trevor."

Jordan frowned, puzzled. Help him? Sure, it was only the thought, but even the thought had never passed through Blair's empty head. "My ex-wife would never have thought of that. Her idea of helping me would be to sit in the family room and manicure her nails while she watched the soaps."

Rosemary smiled. "So, how did that help you?"

"Kept her out of my way while she waited for the cleaning lady to arrive."

Rosemary giggled. In fact, she giggled so enthusiastically that he couldn't help but think she'd known someone very much like his ex-wife.

"It's okay." He chuckled. "I forgive you for not spending your time manicuring your nails. As a guest, you get an A plus. It's downright nice, coming home to a clean house and a hot meal."

"It's the least I can do after imposing on you like this."

"That's all right. You couldn't help it." He paused to dish up potatoes and pour gravy over them.

They chatted sporadically through most of the meal. Rosemary was a charming young woman, but so far she'd learned a lot more about him than he'd learned about her.

"What about your own work? You're a single mother. You must have a job somewhere to support yourself and Trevor. Or are you independently wealthy? If not, who looks after Trevor while you work? Or do you hire a nanny? How did you get time off for this trip?"

His real question, the unspoken one was *why are you here?*

He'd become increasingly curious about that. Oh, yes, she'd been caught in a blizzard, but why was she roaming the back roads of southern Alberta with a baby to begin with? The only game in town here was ranching. And oil.

Rosemary stood to take an apple pie from the oven. "I'm self-employed." She set the pie on the counter.

Jordan smelled its rich aroma with pleasure, but he didn't stop his questioning. "I see. Just what are you self-employed at?"

Rosemary swung to face him, hands on hips. "I'm an independent marketing consultant."

"That sounds like it could be anything. Or nothing. Exactly what does an independent marketing consultant do?"

She leaned back against the kitchen counter and folded her arms. "How about an example?" She looked around. "Say you wanted to start a bed and breakfast—first I'd do research. Does the area have potential for tourism? How many similar services already exist? I'd advise you about how many clients you could comfortably handle, and I'd guide you through the bureaucratic red tape. Then I'd put ads in travel magazines and on the Internet to appeal to people who want to experience ranch life. We'd discuss menus, and whether you should offer extras. Trail rides? Hikes? Hay rides? Get the picture?"

"I see." He paused, then grinned. "If I ever decide to start a bed and breakfast, I'll let you know. And does this leave you with enough time to look after a kid?"

"I run the business from home, but Trevor does take up a lot of my time. I now work much more in the evenings than I used to. But since I don't have much of a social life left anyway, I guess it isn't a big deal." She shrugged. "I'm very lucky. Not all single mothers are able to work at home."

She turned away to cut the pie and to place the dirty dishes into the dishwasher while she chattered on. "What about this area? What kind of services are there for single mothers? Are there daycares with pick-up and drop-off service?"

At it again, was she? She sure asked some strange questions. Could he hire help? Did he have close relatives? What was the local daycare situation? What was the woman up to? Was she on the hunt for a rich Alberta rancher? If so, she was tough out of luck this time.

"I don't think so." He fought to keep his cool and

answer her question about daycare. "Though I never really thought about it, since I don't have any children. And you won't be here long enough for it to matter."

She mumbled into the dishwasher, "I was just trying to make conversation."

"Your ideas of conversation are pretty odd. Ever hear about the weather as something to talk about? We've got plenty of that." He got to his feet. "And now, if you'll excuse me, I have to get busy. I'll have my pie later."

She stepped in front of him to bar him from the door. "Just a minute. Talking about work—the business I was telling you about—I can't run it without my computer, and my computer's still in my car, along with my clothes, Trevor's clothes, and most of Trevor's diapers. Luckily I use cloth ones, or we'd have looked disaster in the face before now."

Diapers? Sure, he'd known Trevor still wore diapers, but he'd never stopped to really think about it. Never stopped to notice that Trevor wore the same clothes every day. That Rosemary wore the same clothes every day, which was why she wore shorts. He'd ignored everything but making sure his wide-ranging cattle survived.

"All right." He stepped past her, placing one hand on the door knob. "I can't bring all your clothes, but I can pick up the computer. It's in a protective case?" He paused. "You planning to run your business from here?"

"Well, if I'm going to be here any longer, I need to get some work done."

"All right. Where is it?"

"In the trunk. A few of Trevor's clothes and some diapers are in a small blue bag beside it. I can get along a few more days if I have to. But—I locked the key in the car. Remember?"

Maybe he should try to be friendlier, more helpful. She seemed awfully nice, even if some of her questions were a little strange. Besides, in a few more days she'd be gone. In the meantime, it wouldn't hurt him to be pleasant.

He grinned at her. "We cowboys can handle those things—given the right tools and more time than we had the other day."

She grinned back. "If you can manage to sleep in

22

until six thirty tomorrow morning, I'll cook you breakfast."

****

True to his word, Jordan came in for breakfast promptly at six-thirty, striding in from the outside door. Rosemary was taking fresh muffins out of the oven, bacon was crackling in the pan, and the red light on the machine showed the coffee was ready.

"Mmm. Smells good." He wore his outdoor clothes and stamped snow from his feet, then set down the objects he'd been carrying.

Rosemary smiled at him. "I didn't mean you had to do a day's work before breakfast."

"I didn't. Just brought the computer and the diapers you asked for."

She was touched and surprised. "How thoughtful! Thanks. Now I'll dish up some food, if you can take off your coat long enough to eat."

She poured coffee, then broke three eggs and slipped them into the pan beside the bacon. "Start on coffee and muffins, while I finish the eggs."

As he sipped coffee and ate bacon and eggs, he gave her a friendly smile. "I'm curious. You've been asking me a lot of questions."

"Never mind. Maybe they were inappropriate. I've decided to take your advice and chat about the weather."

He reached for a muffin. "First, I have a question of my own. Why are you here?"

"Uh." Her mind raced for an answer. "Because of the weather. You know. The storm. I got lost in the storm. You know that."

"I know that. But why were you on the country road to begin with? What are you doing in Alberta?"

She hesitated. What should she say now? She'd intended to observe him for longer before she spoke, but he'd asked a direct question. She'd never been a good liar. She took a deep breath, then plowed ahead. "The truth is, I'm looking for Trevor's father. I understand he lives in this area. I think it's time for Trevor to know him."

"I see." It was obvious from the look on his face that he didn't see at all. Didn't believe her. "You think he lives around here? How likely is that?"

She shoved her plate to the side. "I think I missed a turn somewhere because of the storm and ended up on the wrong road."

"You didn't really answer my question. Do you think Trevor's father lives around here?"

She swallowed, then made up her mind. It was time to forget all the caution and the waiting. Jordan seemed like a good man. It was time to gamble. "All right. The truth. The whole truth. I am looking for Trevor's father, and, yes, I've found him. Jordan, Trevor is your son."

****

Jordan choked on the mouthful of coffee he'd begun to swallow. He sprang to his feet so suddenly that he knocked over the chair he'd been sitting on.

She had to be kidding!

Didn't he wish? He'd give anything if Trevor were his son. But he wasn't. He turned abruptly to Rosemary, arms folded across his chest, feet apart as if preparing for a fight. "You're lying."

Rosemary jumped to her own feet, hands on hips, and glared at him. "How dare you? How dare you call me a liar?"

"Maybe because you are. I might not have a fancy university education, but I've lived my whole life on a ranch. I know where babies come from and how, and I know I can't possibly have one. So what's your game?"

Her look of outrage almost convinced him of her innocence. Almost. You'd think he'd have learned about women. But he'd liked this one with her streaked light-brown hair, her velvet skin, her gray eyes as clear and honest-looking as April rain.

Anyway, this sure changed his plans for breakfast conversation. He'd intended to find out how she came to be on this road, what she was doing, who she was looking for. Those questions had all been answered in a hurry. The new question was *why*.

Were she and Blair in this together? Early in their marriage he'd told Blair how badly he wanted a child. She'd told him she couldn't have children. Certain ingredients went into making a kid. A combination of celibacy and a sterile ex-wife were not among them.

Besides, the sterile ex-wife had walked out almost

two years ago.

The odor of hot buttered muffins teased him, reminded him of the wonderful meals Rosemary cooked. A wave of nausea swept over him, but not from hunger.

He forced himself to speak calmly, his anger trembling just below the surface. "What do you mean, Trevor's my kid? The old story about a one-night stand when we were both drunk after some crowded party? One I don't even remember?"

She stared at him and shook her head vigorously.

He plowed on relentlessly. "Or were you a masked woman I picked up on Halloween night? Why are you doing this? Are you looking for money? What kind of scam are you running?"

"No scam at all." Rosemary's back was straight, her voice angry. She looked mad enough to fling her cup at him, coffee and all, but instead she breathed deeply and ran her fingers around the rim of the mug. "Trevor's your son, but he's not mine. You're right; we've never met. But he *is* your son. That's why I came here."

"Listen, lady." He reached out to grab her upper arm, then thought better of it. She could also make money by suing him if he touched her. "Look at me."

"I already am looking at you, waiting breathlessly for your next words."

Jordan breathed deeply, stared into her eyes, and continued. "Just in case you've never studied biology, I cannot possibly have a son. I cannot possibly have a kid of any kind. So take your dog and pony show somewhere else and find another sucker. I haven't been with a woman since my wife left me. Almost two years ago."

"Exactly. About six months before Trevor was born. He's sixteen months old now." She returned to her chair. "So sit down, shut up, and listen."

Jordan picked up the chair and sat. He pushed pieces of egg around his plate with a piece of toast, then stopped pretending to eat. "I'd trade everything I own for a little guy like your Trevor, but that doesn't mean I'm going to let you con me."

"I am not conning you."

"Yeah," he said. "As soon as this storm's over, I'll have Trevor and me tested, and we'll see who's telling the truth. They can do that now, you know, with DNA testing."

"I know. You do that. I'm not afraid of the results."

"I'll do it. You can depend on it. Now, just how do you fit into all this?"

"Blair's my sister."

There it was. He pushed back his chair and looked sharply at Rosemary. The pieces slid into place. He'd studied her, trying to figure out where he'd seen her. Why hadn't it hit him before? Except for coloring, Blair and Rosemary looked alike. "You said your last name was Robbins. That wasn't her last name. How can you be sisters?" He glanced at her left hand. "Or are you married?"

She shook her head. "No. She changed her name. She never mentioned me? Never mentioned having a sister?"

In spite of everything, he grinned. He couldn't help it. "Yeah," he admitted. "She did mention a sister, but her name wasn't Rosemary. It was Ms. Prim Goody Two Shoes."

"Oh." Rosemary's anger cracked, and she snickered. "I guess that's me."

She drew her hand across her mouth as though to wipe the smile off her face. "Blair was always a wild child. As soon as she turned eighteen, she ran away to be an actress, and changed her name from Tina Robbins to Blair Bellevue."

"Yes. That was her name when I met her."

"After she left you, she came to me, even though we hadn't seen each other for years—hadn't corresponded except for Christmas cards. She was pregnant, and after she finished being pregnant she was a single mother. In any case, she couldn't work. She could party, but she couldn't work. She ate my food and expected me to wait on her until about two months ago. At first, I was almost relieved when she found a new man and disappeared for a quickie divorce. Or didn't you know about that either?"

"Yes." His voice was cold. "I knew about that. Her lawyer notified me. You're not lying about the divorce, but you are lying about the child. Surely you were aware that your sister is sterile."

"What! Are you crazy?" She thumped her coffee mug

onto the table and grasped the edge of the table so tightly that her clenched knuckles stood out white against the oak wood. "Are we talking about two different women?"

"I don't think so. Your sister's name is Blair. My wife's name was Blair. Same woman. You even look alike, except that she's dark and you're blonde."

"Blair is not sterile." Rosemary slammed one fist down on the table so hard that the dishes rattled. "If you'd said some other man was the father, I might have believed you. She has the morals of an alley cat." She slowed her speech, pronouncing the words deliberately, pausing between each one. "But there is absolutely no doubt that Blair is Trevor's mother."

She took a deep breath. "I know. She lived with me, and she wasn't pretending with a balloon under her maternity dress either. I suffered through her morning sickness, I held her hand during her labor pains, and I witnessed Trevor's birth."

"Maybe you're lying about all this. Maybe Trevor really is *your* baby and you're desperately looking for a sucker to become his father."

"I am not lying." The anger was back.

"Yeah. Somebody is."

"Maybe it was Blair." She stuck her chin out, as if challenging him to deny it. "Has that occurred to you? Maybe she lied when she said she was sterile."

Jordan looked up, startled. The idea had never occurred to him. "Why would she do that? She didn't want children. Why should she tell me something that meant we didn't use birth control? Why would a woman who didn't want children have done that?"

"Maybe she did use birth control, and you didn't know. Maybe it was her way of keeping you from asking for children?"

"I don't know." His voice was slow and puzzled. "Unless you're making the whole thing up, it's very strange."

"Yes, it is very strange." She paused and tented her hands under her chin. "But there are women who think they're sterile and aren't. Surely you've heard the stories about the couples who give up and adopt, and the wife immediately becomes pregnant. Did she give you any details?"

He shrugged. "Something about tubes."

"Well, maybe they were almost blocked or whatever, but not quite."

"That's one explanation," Jordan said. "The other one is that you're lying."

Chapter Three

Jordan left the table and stomped out of the house. He had to take care of his cattle, and he had to think about what Rosemary had said. At least, he now understood why she'd asked all the questions about hired men and relatives and daycare. Whether she was lying or whether she wasn't, she expected to leave Trevor with him. Was Trevor her own child and she was looking for a way to dump him? Was she looking for a husband for herself as well as a father for her child?

Or had Blair lied to him, meaning that he could be Trevor's father? Still not a large chance, because, as Rosemary had admitted, Blair had the morals of an alley cat.

Much as he'd like to, he didn't believe Rosemary. He couldn't. If only she'd go and take Trevor with her. Get out of his life, before their leaving cut away a piece of his heart.

But they couldn't travel yet. The storm continued to howl, and snow still covered the roads. He had his cattle to care for and feed until they could get back to green grass and pasture. No time to worry about the two people who'd blown in like autumn leaves into a ditch.

Not that he didn't want the kid. But there was no way he'd be suckered again—especially not by a woman who looked so much like his ex-wife. Blair's hair had been dark, her eyes brown. Rosemary's hair was the color of golden wheat sheaves mixed with stems of sun-bleached hay, her eyes as gray and dusky as wood smoke. But they were both tall and slender. Both had the same upward tilt to their noses, the same generous mouth, the same classy cheekbones.

Blair had been all sweetness and light when they'd met and married, when she'd thought ranch life would be nothing but parties and parades and big checks from the oil company. She'd seen him as a romantic figure in silver-studded leather chaps and vest and bright embroidered satin shirt, riding his prize quarter-horse stallion in the parade at the Calgary Stampede.

He didn't want to cut a romantic figure. He wanted to be a father.

During the brief moments he'd held Trevor, he'd secretly hoped he'd have time to play with the child before they left. He couldn't now. He couldn't afford to get attached to this baby until he found out just what was going on.

Not that he'd have much chance, anyway. Trevor was always asleep when he got up and was down for the night long before he returned.

****

Rosemary picked up her computer and Trevor's bag from the doorway where Jordan had left them. Now that he'd brought her computer, she could catch up with her own work, before she found herself back in Winnipeg without clients.

The room at the end of the bedroom wing held a sofa bed and a desk with an extension telephone on it—the perfect spot for an office. She set up her laptop, then got to work, checking her email and responding, updating client files. Her fingers flew over the keys. She also e-mailed her parents, hoping to reach them before they found out she'd left Winnipeg and began to worry. She gave them an account of the last few days and reminded them to tell no one where she had gone.

When Trevor awoke and demanded his breakfast, she fed him and played with him, then during his mid-morning nap, she went back to her work.

****

By eleven o'clock, Jordan couldn't stand it any more and returned to the house. He strode inside and paced up and down the family room. Rosemary was nowhere to be seen. "Rosemary." He shouted the name. Maybe he'd been lucky and she'd gone. Hah! She couldn't. Sure enough, in a moment she emerged from the hall.

"Where's Trevor?"

"Napping. Thanks for bringing my computer. I've been working on my files. I'll get Trevor up for lunch shortly." She flopped into one of the leather recliners.

"Yeah. Thought of any more lies."

"I just told you what happened. If you want the truth, I was glad when Blair took off and left Trevor behind. She was a horrible mother. And who knows whether you're any better?" She paused and fiddled with the band of her watch. "I still haven't decided on that part of it."

"So then why'd you bring him here?"

She sat up straight, and stared at him like a cat getting ready to spit. "I brought him here because I hoped you could take care of him, love him, be good to him." She gazed at the floor beside him. "Because I hoped that you would keep him safe. I wish I could keep him myself," she added fiercely.

"Then why didn't you? If you're telling me the truth, why didn't you keep him? I didn't even know he existed."

"Because it was the right and honest thing to do."

"Yeah. Be careful you don't choke on your self-righteousness."

Rosemary stood up. "I'm not hungry, but I'll make lunch for you." She stalked into the kitchen, Jordan close behind her.

"Don't bother. I'm not hungry either. Now why did you bring Trevor here?"

She side-stepped the question. "I'd do anything to keep Trevor safe. He's lived with me ever since he was born."

Trevor cried.

"Excuse me." Rosemary's voice was little more than a whisper. She tore her gaze from Jordan, and turned toward the bedroom. "Trevor needs me. He's teething."

He watched her go, watched the swing of her hips in her shorts, the length of leg, the shapely figure. *Dammit.* He liked her, even lusted after her a bit. Why should he feel that way about this particular woman? A woman he'd known only three days. He was a fool. That's why.

Obviously, he'd been without a woman too long.

He'd have to watch himself, before he became putty in this one's hands. Before he started to believe her lies.

Rosemary returned with Trevor in her arms.

"Uncah," Trevor babbled, waving his hands at Jordan. "Uncah."

A wave of longing washed over Jordan as he looked

at the baby. He didn't dare hope that Trevor belonged to him. He couldn't see a resemblance. Trevor had brown eyes. His own were blue. His hair was jet black. His skin, if not bronzed by the sun and wind, would be fair. Irish coloring. Trevor's hair was dark brown, his skin tinted golden by the hand of nature. *No.* Wishful thinking didn't produce babies.

But he remembered his own mother had light brown hair and brown eyes. And Blair's eyes were brown. Was it possible that Blair had lied to him? That Rosemary had told the truth? That Trevor might be his son?

But why would Blair have lied about that particular thing? Maybe to keep him from badgering her about having children, like Rosemary had suggested. He had to admit, that was the sort of thing Blair would do.

Jordan watched Rosemary open the fridge, then rub something over the baby's gums. Then she poured milk into a glass, and held it to Trevor's lips. The child slurped the milk greedily, blowing bubbles as he drank. Rosemary set the empty glass down, then leaned against the counter and rubbed his shoulder with her forehead until he shrieked with glee.

If she didn't love the child, she could qualify for an Oscar. Jordan tried to visualize Blair with a child in her arms. The image wouldn't come. Blair dancing, laughing, teasing—yes. But never with a child. Not that he hadn't entertained this perfect-family fantasy during the first year of their marriage until Blair had dropped her bomb and blown his fantasy out of the water.

Maybe Rosemary was telling the truth and maybe she wasn't. At the moment, he'd let her know he didn't intend to be a pushover.

"Now listen to me." Jordan glared at her. "You see this house? Of course, you see this house. You've been living in it for several days. Nice house, isn't it?"

"Yes. It's a very nice house."

"A very nice house. In fact, you might just be coveting this very nice house."

"Uh—no." Rosemary shook her head. "I've enjoyed being here. I haven't even minded dusting it, but I haven't exactly been coveting it."

"Yeah? Well, just in case you get those ideas, I'll tell

you a bit about it. Bring the kid into the family room and sit down."

Rosemary followed him dutifully and plunked into a recliner with Trevor on her lap.

Jordan paced up and down the rug. "It hasn't always been this nice. My great-grandfather built it as a two-bedroom log cabin, and generation by generation it's been expanded and improved. The improvements your sister made were cosmetic—bathrooms and decks and new furniture. In fact the only original furniture left is what's in here and my mother's piano. I wouldn't let her get rid of that. And I wouldn't let her redecorate the room we're in now, the main part of the original cabin."

He paused in front of her and spread his hands. "This house is my heritage—my parents', my grandparents'. It's more than a color-coordinated laundry and a Jacuzzi. When I can no longer run the ranch, it will go to strangers. Until then, I'm going to hold up my end of my heritage."

"I understand." Rosemary sounded puzzled. "But why are you telling me all this?"

"Just to show you that this place has been in my family for four generations. I have no intention of letting you, or any other fast-talking snake-oil peddler, continue to erode it. I'm not letting you sell me a fake son to be the fifth generation." He turned abruptly and spoke over his shoulder. "Excuse me, it's time to get back to work."

****

Jordan strode off, leaving Rosemary gaping after him. Rude? That put it mildly. Or was it rudeness? The catch in Jordan's voice as he broke off? If she stretched her imagination a bit, she could almost believe he'd been overcome with emotion as he described his feelings for his family home. Could almost believe he'd turned away so she couldn't see his tears.

A proud man would do that. An honest man couldn't fake it.

It looked more and more as if Jordan Sterling was a man she could trust. And that was all very nice, but Trevor's father would also need reliable child care. That is, once he was convinced he was Trevor's father.

She believed Jordan about Blair's extravagance. In

the year and a half Blair had lived with her, she'd never offered to split the rent, never come home with an armful of groceries, never brought Trevor a new toy. Yet she bought new clothes for herself—expensive new clothes.

When Rosemary had suggested Blair share household expenses, she'd been met with blunt refusal— the *how could you possibly expect me—a poor single mother* line. For Trevor's sake, Rosemary had backed down.

If she'd thrown her out, Blair might have taken Trevor with her. Then who would have loved him and taken proper care of him? Who could have protected him against Blair and the uncles?

When Blair found the new man she married, or at least she said she'd married him, she abandoned Trevor completely, and Rosemary became, in fact if not in name, Trevor's mother. Their father, Blair's and Rosemary's, was a doctor in a small town north of Winnipeg, a trusted and respected man in his community, so, at least, Rosemary had the emotional support of family, and Trevor knew his grandparents.

But now Blair had returned. Then one night Rosemary had overheard a phone conversation and her world had turned upside down. Blair was planning to sell Trevor. That's when Rosemary had grabbed Trevor and fled into the night. Blair had every legal right to the child. Sure, Rosemary could go to the police with her story, but she had no proof. She'd probably be laughed out of the police station at best—at worst, charged with kidnapping.

Rosemary tucked her feet under her in the big leather chair and pondered. Jordan gave the impression of being a good man—a responsible hard-working man, attached to his land and his roots. She couldn't hold his attitude toward herself against him. She'd be skeptical too if a stranger came to her house, with a baby and no apparent destination in mind.

At least thanks to the storm, she couldn't go anywhere yet. She had more time to convince Jordan that Trevor was his. As far as telling him the rest, well, she'd watch and wait.

Blair had told her little about the ranch except that it was lonely and boring and she sure didn't intend to be

34

stuck there with a kid for the rest of her life. Rosemary looked out the window at the expanse of snow-covered pastures, of the dim shape of the Rockies towering in the background. It didn't look boring to her.

And neither did Jordan Sterling. She recalled his lanky powerful body, his gaze as blue and cutting as diamond chips. She shook her head. What a lot of nonsense. She turned the page on her thoughts. She wasn't here to rank Jordan Sterling on sex appeal—just on fatherhood qualities. Her next job was to convince him that he really was Trevor's father.

****

Rosemary glanced at the kitchen clock, a polished pine plank cut in the shape of a cowboy riding a bucking bronco. Three-thirty. The storm had blown over as suddenly as it began. From the kitchen window, Rosemary viewed a dazzling world of ivory snow and crystal ice, all sparkling in fresh sunshine under a blue mid-afternoon sky. The birch trees beyond the back patio shimmered under their weight of diamonds, displaying more finery than a princess bride.

Only three days ago she'd arrived here in a blinding snowstorm. In that short time, this house had begun to feel like home. How could she possibly convince Jordan to care for Trevor? She shut her eyes and visualized the worst possible scenario—Blair finding out where they were, and the police coming to remove Trevor from her and return him to his biological mother. The woman who would then cross the border and sell him.

The very thought made Rosemary's blood run cold.

She returned to her improvised office and her computer, and lost herself in her work. When she felt frozen to her chair and her fingers were stiff, she stood to stretch and look around the room. Just out of curiosity, she slid open a mirrored closet door. Clothes. Women's clothes. So many that they packed the long closet, many of them looking brand new.

These clothes would solve Rosemary's immediate problem. Blair and she were the same size. She riffled through the closet. Long gowns. Short party dresses. Slinky pant suits. Where had Blair worn this stuff? Why had she left it all behind? Had she left in a rush? Or wouldn't she be caught dead wearing last year's styles?

Rosemary paused, her hand resting on a deep rose jumpsuit that looked like silk. She took the hanger from the rod and examined the garment. According to the tag it was man-made fabric, washable.

She shrugged, took off her shorts and top, and, slowly, luxuriously, eased on the jumpsuit. It fit snugly around her waist, showed off her bust, ballooned like harem pants around her legs. Yes, it was impractical to wear around the house, but she was irresistibly tempted. At least she could wash it if she spilled tomato sauce on it. She'd be very careful to keep it clean and would take it off before Jordan got home.

Unfortunately, he came back early.

****

When Jordan entered the kitchen, dusk was settling in. The only light turned on was the one over the kitchen stove.

Jordan blinked, paused, and blinked again.

Blair. Blair stood silhouetted in front of the kitchen stove. She wore the outfit he had bought for her when he first met her, now years ago. It had looked beautiful on her then, and it looked beautiful on her now.

"Hi. You're back early. We're having beef stroganoff, but I haven't started the pasta. It'll be half an hour or so."

He blinked the third time, and the woman in front of him was no longer Blair, but Rosemary. Of course. In the dim light, they looked alike. Somewhere, Rosemary had found that pantsuit and discovered a way to get out of the shorts she'd worn nonstop since her arrival.

"No problem." Jordan wasn't hungry yet anyway. "You know, for a minute there, I thought you were Blair. The outfit, I guess."

"I hope you don't mind. You weren't around for me to ask your permission. I'm getting pretty tired of wearing the same shorts everyday."

"No problem." He forced a polite smile. "It was just that I recognized the getup, and in the dim light— you see, just for a moment, I thought, well—"

"That she'd returned like a ghost to haunt you?"

"Well, yes, something like that." He turned away to take off his coat and boots in the entry hall, then came through to the kitchen. He plunked down on a kitchen chair and continued to explain as Rosemary continued dinner preparations. "She got that outfit the day after we met. We were wandering through displays of arts and crafts and through stores. She fell in love with this. I'd fallen in love with her and bought it."

"She was so beautiful." He paused. "She tried that on, and with her dark hair and eyes and complexion—"

"Tell you what," Rosemary said. "Tomorrow I'll wear something with the price tag still on. Then I won't remind you of anything but your charge card."

A shadow crossed his face. "Look, you can wear any of those clothes you want." One side of his mouth quirked up in a half grin. "I don't intend to use them."

Rosemary returned his smile. "I've just finished feeding Trevor, and put him down for the night. He was a little more restless than usual. Probably teeth. But he seems to have settled now."

"Sure," Jordan said. "No rush about dinner. Maybe I'll celebrate the early evening by having a shower and getting into clean clothes. Half an hour, you said?"

Rosemary nodded, and Jordan went to the spare bedroom where he now slept. He showered in the guest bathroom so as not to disturb Trevor. The baby usually slept soundly, but Rosemary had mentioned that he was a bit more restless than usual.

He put on clean jeans, then rummaged through the few clothes he'd transferred into the guest room closet. He could find only heavy work shirts and tonight he'd fancied something lighter. Something more in sync with a leisurely dinner and an evening spent relaxing.

He knew exactly where to find the shirt he wanted. He'd tiptoe in and get it. His comings and goings had never disturbed Trevor before.

Since Rosemary and Trevor began using the room, he'd plugged in a night light that gave him plenty of light to find his way around. He glanced over at Trevor.

The baby had crawled out from under the covers and lay on top of the pillow, his head turned to one side, his little rear end sticking up, and his legs out behind him. He wore only a shirt and diaper. Probably Rosemary tried to make his few clothes go as far as possible. Even with the small bag he'd brought her along with the computer, Trevor still wasn't exactly the best-dressed baby in the West.

Jordan stepped closer to the bed, then stood looking down on him for a moment. Should he tuck him back under the covers? That might disturb him. Just leave him be. Maybe tell Rosemary that he was uncovered.

His heart beat a little faster. Trevor was a beautiful baby. He'd give anything if Rosemary's story was true. He just stood there a moment, coveting the child and dreaming. A baby to die for. Brown hair. Flawless skin. Little arms spread-eagled to either side. Legs, bent at the knees, ending in pink and perfect feet

Jordan stared at those feet. It couldn't be!

Tentatively, gently, he touched the toes. Ran his fingers as lightly as the touch of a feather over the ends of them.

It couldn't be!

He counted. He stared again. He counted again.

It couldn't be, but it was.

On each of those pink and perfect feet, Trevor had six toes.

****

Jordan stared at Trevor a moment longer before he turned away.

A son. He really and truly had a son. No doubts left. Having six toes was genetic, and too rare to be coincidence. His father had had normal feet, but his grandfather and one uncle had each had six toes—like himself and Trevor.

What should he do now? He couldn't possibly face Rosemary yet, and admit that he'd wronged her with his suspicions. Or maybe he hadn't. She could still be running a scam—alone or with Blair. Right now, he had to get a grip on himself and look at the situation from every possible angle.

Rosemary had said dinner wouldn't be ready for half an hour. That might give him time to get his emotions under control enough to behave normally. He put on the shirt he'd come for, and walked through the family room, and into the kitchen. Keeping his back to Rosemary, he sidled across the room and into the entry hall, then mumbled as he reached for his coat. "I just remembered there's something I have to do in the barn."

The barn was dark and silent except for the muted noises of the animals. Jordan flicked on the main lights and entered, then closed the door behind him.

Satan and Ranger greeted him with soft nickers. The two dogs bounded to his feet, wagging their tails to get his attention. The black and white cat, yellow eyes glowing, sneered at him from the hay bale where she lay.

Jordan stood in front of Satan and took the horse's face in his hands. Satan nosed his jacket, looking for an apple or a carrot. "Sorry fella." Jordan moved his hands up to fondle the animal's ears. "Nothing for you tonight. Except news. I've got a son." He leaned his forehead on Satan's face and heard his voice tremble with emotion. "You know that cute kid we brought home in the storm that day? He's mine." He moved to Ranger and stroked the blaze down the bay's face and the white velvety nose. "A son," he told the horse. "I have a son."

The two farm dogs followed him and now sat at his feet and whined, looking up at him with beseeching eyes. He turned away from Ranger and patted them, first one and then the other. The barn cat ignored him, but he picked her up and ruffled her silky fur anyway. "Did you hear that, Pretty Paws? I've got an honest to goodness son." The cat squirmed so he put her down. She jumped from the hay bale to the floor and stalked off into the dark corners of the barn, her tail held high and twitching indignantly. Apparently mice were better company than human fathers.

Jordan punched one fist into the air, like a hockey player who's just scored a goal. "Yes," he shouted, his voice echoing hollowly in the empty spaces of the barn. "Yes, I have a son!"

He slumped down on the hay bale vacated by Pretty Paws.

So, he'd wanted to be a father.

He wasn't the last Sterling any more. The ranch could stay in the family forever. Trevor could grow up here, learn to ride, share the running of the ranch with him, eventually take over. And after Trevor, Trevor's kids.

Jordan could feel his heart expanding in his chest,

pushing against his ribs and breastbone. He felt like he was about to explode with joy and pride. Trevor was such a neat little guy. Jordan had fallen in love with the child the first time he'd seen him, had felt a surge of tenderness when the small body lay packaged between himself and Rosemary on the cold trip home.

And now? This little guy he'd fallen in love with from the very moment he'd looked into the back seat of Rosemary's car and seen the soft cheek resting on the car-seat was actually his. *His* baby.

The big question was how would Jordan take care of a child? If Rosemary turned out to be legit, would she possibly agree to stay on for awhile until he could find child care? He could hardly blame her if she wouldn't, not after the way he'd treated her and doubted her.

His thoughts rambled back to Blair. Pretty Paws reminded him of Blair's softer gentler side. Blair had found her as a kitten in an animal shelter. Her first words had been, "Ooh, isn't that one lovely? Black with white trim and those darling white socks. Can I have her, Jordan? Please. I'm going to name her Pretty Paws."

And, yes, Blair got the kitten, as she got everything she wanted. He remembered her, sitting by the fire watching television, stroking the kitten and ruffling her fur while the kitten kneaded Blair's jeans-covered legs with her snow-white paws. That had been one of the few times he'd almost loved Blair, even after the first flush of passion had faded.

Pretty Paws had been a housecat then, and Jordan had to admit she'd been a very well-behaved one. But when Blair left, there was no time in Jordan's life for pampered pets. She'd had to join the dogs in the barn and earn her keep by catching mice. He levered himself from the hay bale and prepared to deal with the here and now.

Chapter Four

The next morning, Rosemary had the eggs for omelets scrambled, waiting for Jordan to appear.

He'd seemed odd last evening, ever since he'd left the kitchen to change his clothes, then rushed to the barn. When he came back he didn't really look at her, but there'd been a submerged excitement about him, so much so that while he ate she checked on Trevor to be sure he was all right. He had crawled from under the covers, but was sleeping peacefully, a sweet baby smile on his face.

She heard Jordan now, his steps coming down the hall from the bedroom wing. When he entered the room, he looked at her. "Good morning. You look nice."

She wore a long denim skirt and a blue cashmere sweater. Not kitchen duds, but a big improvement over the shorts and less flamboyant than the rose-colored pantsuit.

"Thank you." She smiled at his compliment. "I'll have omelets ready in a minute. Cheese and onion okay?"

"Great." He took his place at the table.

She looked at him. He still had the strange aura about him she'd noticed last night. Hopefully he wasn't a schizophrenic in one of his murderous moods. She smiled to herself. Not likely, or he'd have murdered Blair long ago. She served up the omelets and toast, poured two cups of coffee, and sat down opposite him.

He ate quickly, then gazed at her thoughtfully. "Rosemary, we have to talk."

She put down her piece of toast. What on earth coming now? "All right. What do you want to talk about?"

"Trevor. Trevor really is my son, isn't he? You weren't lying." Rosemary felt herself go white, and held her crossed hands to her throat.

"Yes, he is, but you were so sure he wasn't. What changed your mind?"

"He was lying on top of the pillow when I went in to

41

get a shirt last night. He wasn't covered up. He has six toes."

"Yes? So?"

"I have six toes too." Ah. Now she understood. There was so much emotion in his expression, she couldn't help but smile. "So did my grandfather and one of my uncles."

A few seconds later he continued. "I believe that Trevor is my son. I'm delighted, but I still don't understand why you acted the way you did. Why did you wait four days to tell me?"

"I wanted to decide whether you'd be a good father to him. And I still don't know that for sure. But you just kept at me about why I was here, and I couldn't stand lying anymore, so I told you."

"All right. Next question. Why did you come here with him? Why didn't you just keep him, like you said you wanted to? And not that cock and bull story about it being the right thing to do."

"Jordan?" She moved to touch him, then snatched her hand back. "You will keep Trevor? You have to. Yes, I had another reason, besides the cock and bull story, as you called it. There's something else I have to tell you."

"Go on."

The lump in her throat threatened to choke her. The thought of what she had to tell him was about to make her erupt in tears. "I didn't just bring him because I wanted you to know each other, like I said at first." She turned the spoon over on the table and rubbed the bowl with her thumb. "Trevor's in danger, terrible danger. Blair ran away with a man, like I said. She claims they're married. She just left Trevor with me. She didn't sign anything, not for me or my parents. We couldn't do anything without contacting her, and we didn't even know where to start looking.

"Then, a couple weeks ago, she phoned and asked me if she could come to visit Trevor. I didn't see how I could refuse, so I invited her to stay with me."

She felt as if her lips were frozen, but she continued. "I was working at the computer late one night with Trevor asleep in his crib beside me. Blair had just come home and was in my bedroom next door. I wanted to call a customer, but when I picked up the phone, Blair was on the line, talking to a man. They were talking about Trevor, about selling him for two hundred thousand dollars."

She dabbed at the tears scalding her cheeks. "I didn't know what to do or where to go. Trevor is legally Blair's. So after she hung up, I waited long enough to be sure she was asleep, then I grabbed my computer, some clothes, and ran. I didn't know where to go, so I thought of you. You're his father. You have a legal right to keep him."

"Couldn't you have gone to the police?" His voice sounded hopeful.

Did he really think it was that simple? "I honestly don't know. I couldn't take the chance. I don't have any proof. She's his mother, and she has his birth certificate. Once she had him across the border she could do as she pleased. The customs officers wouldn't know that she wasn't planning to bring him back."

The color drained from Jordan's face and his eyes turned cold, but he remained silent.

Rosemary picked up her paper napkin, shredding it as she talked. "Jordan, they were going to sell him. They were going to sell Trevor. Don't you understand? To strangers. I'd have never seen him... Never... I..." She threw down the remnants of the napkin and broke into sobs, burying her face in her hands.

He waited till her sobs had subsided then asked. "Why didn't you tell me this part of it before?"

She shook her head and spoke through her fingers. "I couldn't. If you refused to believe me about being his father, then I'd have had to keep running. If the DNA test showed you weren't his father, would you have rejected him then, and contacted Blair?"

"Didn't it occur to you that if you'd told me all this to begin with I'd have kept and protected him no matter whose child he was?"

She shook her head violently and looked up at him. "I couldn't take the chance."

Jordan reached across the table and took one of her hands in both of his, clutching it so tightly she yelped. He relaxed his grip, but kept her hand sheltered in his as she told him about her flight, the dark, the storm, the nightmare quality of the whole two days.

43

Jordan squeezed her hand once more before he released it. "I'll talk to my lawyer and see what my legal options are. I'll have him contact your lawyer and start collecting all the information we can to prove she's an unfit mother. I don't know about tracing phone calls that are two weeks old and that sort of thing. But they'll know—the lawyers. I'll hire a private investigator if necessary. I'll take care of everything."

The weight of fear and anxiety that had burdened Rosemary's soul for the last several days lifted and blew away like the clouds of last week's storm.

"That's what I hoped. That's why I came." She pressed her hands between her knees to keep them from shaking. "I know she's my sister, but she's an evil woman, Jordan. I'd never realized until that awful night just how evil."

He grinned wryly. "Well, I didn't know she was that evil either, but I knew she had a love affair with money, especially spending it."

"I'm surprised she didn't end up with half the ranch."

"I was lucky there. My lawyer made me draw up a pre-nuptial agreement before the wedding."

"You *were* lucky. Really lucky. Otherwise she'd have ruined you."

"He's a good lawyer. He'll know what to do and he'll help us."

Silence hung like tree leaves on a windless day.

"I'm sorry I doubted you." Jordan swallowed. "Sorry I suspected you of lying."

Rosemary watched his Adam's apple convulse. Then she looked at her plate. "It's all right. If I'd been in your position, I'd probably have done the same. All that matters now is Trevor."

Jordan slammed the palm of his hand against the table.

"Damn." Then he looked at Rosemary. "Don't worry. I'll take care of Trevor. I'll protect you both." His voice became a whisper. "They won't get away with it. Either of them."

"You'll keep him then?"

"Of course. I intended to ever since I discovered he was mine. I wouldn't have let even you keep him, never mind Blair and one of her million lovers. I spent most of last night going over how I could take care of him."

"And?"

"I love the little guy. I think I did even before I knew he was mine." He hesitated, then continued. "Of course I'm going to keep him. But you've seen how I live here. It won't be easy."

Rosemary buttered a piece of toast, then threw it down on her plate. There was no way she could eat.

"So I want to ask you something. I spent the night psyching myself up to this, and now it's even more important. I guess…I know this is asking a lot. But could you stay on for awhile? Give me a chance to sort out what I can do about daycare or whatever?"

Rosemary paused a moment to take it in.

"I know it's an imposition. I don't blame you if you don't want to do it for me. But maybe you could do it for Trevor."

Rosemary's heart did gymnastics in her chest. A reprieve. She didn't have to part with Trevor. Not yet.

She continued to stare at her food, picking up the discarded piece of toast and folding it over mangled strip of bacon. Then she nibbled at the improvised sandwich.

Jordan took a deep breath. "I'll clear out that room you're using for a study, and I'll take care of the housekeeping and cooking."

Rosemary remembered the frozen steaks and French fries that she suspected made up his total diet before she arrived, and wrinkled her nose mentally.

"You love Trevor. We'll work out some kind of salary for you. The ranch makes money." He grinned wryly. "And the truth is there are a few oil wells scattered around it, and they make money too."

"I'll stay," she said. "For Trevor. And I'll do the cooking and housekeeping—not *Better Homes and Gardens'* housekeeping, but what I've been doing. No salary. Save your spare income for Trevor's education. My business pays very well."

"I know it's a lot to ask. You're a young attractive woman. You should be dating, going to parties."

"Yes." She toyed with the knife at the side of her plate. He thought she was attractive? "I miss those things sometimes. But I didn't have that life in Winnipeg either after Trevor was born. Trevor is far more important to me than dating. I'd like to stay."

"You would?" He sounded almost surprised. "That's great! Then I'll make an appointment with my lawyer as soon as I can. Could you write down names and addresses, and anything else you think of that might help?"

"I'll do it right away." That wasn't all she had to do right away. It was also time to squelch the attraction she was beginning to feel for Jordan.

She'd stay until Jordan found day care for Trevor, and until his lawyer came up with a strategy to keep the child safe. She'd also try to see that Jordan quit working eighteen hours a day. He needed free time. Time to play with his son. Time to relax. He'd said she needed to date and go to parties. Well, she wasn't the only one. Jordan Sterling needed more time for fun, too.

A sound somewhere between a cry and a chuckle reached her ears.

"Trevor's awake." Rosemary pushed back her chair.

"Let me." It seemed that Jordan's shoulders grew wider and his chest expanded. Rosemary poured herself a second cup of coffee and watched Jordan stride from the room.

There was no further noise from the bedroom. Rosemary ate the cold remnants of her omelet and tiptoed down the hall. The door to Jordan's room was ajar. Trevor had gone back to sleep, lying on his back, arms and legs flung out.

Jordan stood beside him, his face in profile to Rosemary, but oblivious to everything, gazing at the child. Rosemary held her breath. Jordan's head was bowed and tears streamed down his face.

Silently Rosemary backed up out of Jordan's range of vision. She tiptoed to the kitchen, sat down and finished her coffee.

Trevor was in good hands. Blair and her husband could never harm him now.

****

When Jordan returned, he had Trevor in his arms. He gazed at his son, but spoke to Rosemary. "Tell you what. The storm's pretty well blown out, and I've finally got the cattle all where they're safe and fed. I think I heard snowplows on the main road late yesterday afternoon. So I'll plow the driveway and bring your car up. Okay? Now that you're staying, you need to have your own things."

"Fine," she said. "And you can vacate the guest digs and move back into your own room. I'll move myself and Trevor into the room with the bunk beds."

"You don't have to do that."

"Yes, I do. When I was just here for a few days, it was different. But now I'm staying for awhile, you need your room back, and I need my own space."

****

Rosemary watched from the living room windows as Jordan backed the pickup with the snowplow blade out of the garage and swung it in a wide circle with a debonair flourish that made her heart race. Not letting herself fall for him was going to be hard. A cowboy hero, driving a pickup truck. He disappeared down the driveway in a shower of snow, while two yellow farm dogs of uncertain breed romped behind him.

She hummed to herself as she dressed and fed Trevor, then held him to the window to watch Jordan and the dogs. Jordan turned the plow around before taking another run at the driveway.

Trevor crowed and waved his arms as he watched the pluming snow. "Uncah," he babbled. "Uncah." And then, "Doggy. Doggy."

The plow and the dogs disappeared from sight.

Trevor turned toward Rosemary. "Aunty Wose." He pummeled her shoulder with his baby fists.

Rosemary held Trevor with one arm, while, with her free hand, she carried an assortment of pots and pans and lids and headed off to the study. Quickly, she moved her few things to her new bedroom and went back to the study and her computer. First, she jotted down the things Jordan had asked for, then copied them out more neatly by hand. In her hurried flight, she hadn't had time or space to bring a printer. Once she finished that, she settled down to keep in touch with her clients.

As Trevor banged lids, and nested pots inside each

other, Rosemary's fingers raced over the computer keys. She heard the pickup come back into the yard, but ignored it.

Later, she heard the sound of a different motor and looked out the window. She saw her own small car idling up the driveway with Jordan at the wheel. His black horse and the two dogs plodded behind.

She scooped Trevor up onto her left hip, and went to the living room to meet Jordan when he came in.

Trevor babbled and waved his arms. "Hossy. Hossy."

Rosemary moved her hip to bounce him. "Yes. Horsy."

"Hossy, Aunty Wose. Scc hossy."

She clutched Trevor more snugly against her. Even if Blair got her own lawyer and fought to get Trevor back, it wouldn't be as easy to take him from his father as from his aunt, especially now that Trevor lived on this remote ranch with his father. Taking him now would involve balancing the laws of one province against the laws of another, and balancing a father whose ancestors had lived on this ranch for generations against a woman who was a drifter and hadn't visited her parents since she left home at the age of eighteen.

And wasn't there some truth in the old saying about possession being nine-tenths of the law? Rosemary squeezed Trevor so hard he yelped. How could she ever give up this precious, precious baby? She was grateful she didn't have to yet.

Jordan stepped out of the car, and started to the house, carrying two suitcases. Rosemary met him at the door.

"Thanks." She took the suitcases and set them on the floor. "Any problem getting into the car?"

"None at all. Amazing what you can do with a coat hanger. I'll get the rest of your things." He turned toward the dogs and nodded first at one, then at the other. "Ben and Buster. They're farm dogs, not house dogs. I kept them inside the barn during the storm. That's why you haven't seen them before. Once they know you they'll protect you with their lives."

She stood in the doorway with Trevor on her hip, and held out one hand. The dogs sniffed at her and at Trevor's feet, then turned to follow their master. Rosemary watched Jordan stride toward the truck, admiring the broad shoulders under the heavy sheepskin coat, the narrow hips encased in skin-tight jeans. Even his worn cowboy boots were sexy.

****

Dinner was over, and the kitchen cleaned. Jordan sat in the family room checking over the information Rosemary had written down for him, while she was curled in the other recliner reading. Trevor lay on his back on a blanket and played with his toes. The perfect family. Trevor kicked his legs and whimpered and held out his arms to Rosemary.

"Bedtime for you, chum." Jordan followed her to the bedroom and watched from the doorway as Rosemary nestled the baby against her, making shushing noises. He still could hardly believe that the baby she was holding was his. A new fantasy invaded his mind. The three of them. Trevor, the baby, himself, the father, and Rosemary, the mother. Both of them in Jordan's arms.

Rosemary shifted her weight from left foot to right, to left, to right, rocking back and forth. Her hips moved provocatively giving Jordan a sensual image of those hips moving against him. *No.* He had no business thinking of her that way. She wasn't really Trevor's mother. Nor his wife. Only in his imagination. The ceiling light shone against her hair, making a golden halo around her head as she continued to rock Trevor. They looked like Madonna and Child.

The scene tore at his heart, and Jordan turned away.

He'd been so shattered when Blair told him she couldn't have children. He'd considered his marriage vows sacred—for better or for worse, till death do us part. After Blair told him she was sterile he knew it was for worse. He'd accepted that he faced an eternity of marriage to a shallow woman, without even a child to make it worthwhile. He'd accepted that the ranch that had been built with sweat and love for four generations would go to strangers. His cousins and second cousins—people he didn't even know—had all gone their distant ways, uninterested in ranches and roots.

Now he stepped out of the doorway and waited down

the hall for Rosemary to lay Trevor on the bottom bunk. A lump lodged in his throat, threatening to choke him with pure joy. His child. His son.

He heard Rosemary's light step, and turned to watch her. She moved toward him and smiled. He looked down at her, at the radiant smile, the golden hair, and inhaled the soft scent of garden flowers that had drifted from her since he'd brought her suitcases. She was so different from her sister. Blair had always worn heavy musky scents that reminded him of smoky rooms and headaches.

And Blair had deserted not only him, but her own child. Rosemary was the one who had brought Trevor to him. Rosemary, the woman as sweet and fragrant as her name.

Against his will, he found himself moving to close the distance between them. He reached out and encircled her with his arms. He bent his head so that his lips hovered a scant inch above hers. The low moan of desire he heard came from his own throat. "Oh, God, Rosemary."

He lowered his lips against hers, and she stiffened in his arms. Would she wriggle away? Slap him? Who could blame her?

But suddenly she relaxed against him. Her body, all curves and softness, lay close to his. The soft surrender of her breasts as they molded themselves against his chest warmed the ice within him.

He moved his lips against hers, nibbling them, planting soft kisses on them and on either side of them. She tasted of chocolate cake. "Rosemary."

Her arms slid up, and wound around his neck. She ran the fingers of one hand through his hair. Then, miracle of miracles, her lips began to move, responding to his, returning his kiss.

She drew away just far enough to stick out the tip of her tongue and tickle the line between his lips. To tease, to tantalize, to invite him to enter her mouth.

No! He drew sharply away. She looked at him in stunned silence, her soft lips still slightly parted.

"I'm sorry," he said hoarsely. "That was out of line. It should never have happened."

She stood, frozen in time like Lot's wife. Her hair shone brighter than new-minted pennies under the hall light. Her gray eyes darkened until they looked almost black. He knew he'd hurt her, but he had no idea what to say to make it better. He only knew he had to get away from her before they did something they'd both regret in the morning.

He turned abruptly and stumbled down the hall to his own room, and thought about how the last twenty-four hours had changed his life.

He had to watch himself. He didn't need, couldn't handle a romantic involvement. She seemed so sweet and innocent, grabbing her in dark corners would drive her away, leaving him with no way to care for Trevor, even short term.

A stab of fear shook his very being, and his mouth went dry with dread.

****

"Go to bed," Jordan had said. Rosemary stumbled into her room, his words ringing in her ears. Which of Jordan Sterling's actions were sincere, the warm and tender kiss, or the withdrawal that followed it?

She stood in the room, listening to Trevor breathing softly in his sleep. She wouldn't be able to sleep for hours. She couldn't turn on the light, or she'd wake Trevor. Softly, she tiptoed to the closet, and opened her suitcase. The only thing left in it after she'd unpacked was the album of baby pictures. She searched it out with her fingertips, clutched it, and closed the case with a soft snick. Then she stole down the hall to the study, sat on the sofa, and turned on the light.

For a moment, she sat with the book on her lap, idly running her fingers over the blue suede cover, down the spine of the back. "Your Baby Boy" slanted across the front in gold-leaf cursive writing.

All she'd have of Trevor before long was in here. No, most likely she wouldn't even have that. She'd probably leave the book with Trevor's father.

She sighed and opened the album. There was Trevor, lying in his basket in the hospital nursery. Even then, the nurses had commented on what a good baby he was, had vied to carry him to his mother's room so they could cuddle him on the way. There was one here of herself holding him in the hospital. One of the nurses had snapped that picture.

Even before that picture was taken, Rosemary had bonded with Trevor.

The story unfolded. Blair putting Trevor's car seat into Rosemary's car for the drive home from the hospital. The next showed Trevor in Rosemary's apartment in his crib in her study. Even then, Blair had had Rosemary's spacious bedroom all to herself. When Trevor cried in the night, Rosemary had gotten out of bed, warmed his bottle, and fed him.

In many cases, Blair knew she'd taken the pictures, but after the initial showing, Rosemary put them away and never brought them out again to remind Blair they existed. She'd sorted and pasted them into the album late at night, then hidden the album. Blair had never asked about the pictures, never asked if she could have copies.

Three full pages showed Trevor's christening. Rosemary had taken him to the church in the rural town north of Winnipeg where her parents lived, since Blair had said she couldn't be bothered with hypocritical out-dated religious rites. Trevor wore the same long white christening gown that had once been Rosemary's. Rosemary played the role of the baby's mother, her own parents standing beside her.

There were a few other pictures in an envelope tucked into the album. These had been surreptitiously taken, of Blair and various and sundry of the uncles dancing to taped music in Rosemary's living room, drinking, laughing. How she'd wanted to throw them all out—every single uncle of them. To threaten them with the police if they refused to go. To lay down the law to Blair telling her she couldn't invite them to the apartment to begin with.

But then, Blair might have stomped out in a rage and, to get revenge, taken Trevor with her. So instead, Rosemary had unobtrusively snapped a few pictures, then hidden out in her own room, trying to close her ears to the noise, and hoping nothing was damaged. Grateful that Trevor was safely in her room with her.

She was glad now she had these pictures. Jordan could use them to show his lawyer, part of the evidence that Blair was an unfit mother.

She closed the book slowly and clutched it to her breasts, leaning forward so that any spilled tears would not fall on the cover. How could she leave her baby? It was the right thing for Jordan. It was the right thing for Trevor. He would be safe on this ranch with a father who would love him, who would put him first in everything regardless of snowstorms and cows and ranches, who would hire the best lawyer money could buy. Trevor was Jordan's fifth generation, his first-born, probably his last.

No, she couldn't be so selfish as to try to keep Trevor to herself. But it hurt—the thought of losing this happy cheerful baby who had belonged to her from the moment he left the hospital.

****

The next morning, Rosemary stood over the stove, dawdling, procrastinating, turning bacon over one strip at a time, breaking eggs into the pan, putting each half shell separately into the garbage. Anything to avoid Jordan's eyes. She had no idea what his kiss of the evening before had been about, but he'd sure made it obvious he regretted it.

She regretted it too. A woman always regretted making a fool of herself. She still feel the imprint of his mouth on hers. She had to face it, admit it. She'd enjoyed his kiss, had been disappointed when it ended.

She knew giving in to her physical desires for Jordan was a bad idea. He'd been smart to quit when he had. Before, when she'd intended to leave soon, it hadn't been that important. Unless something serious developed between the two of them, a few stolen moments of passion wouldn't have mattered one way or the other—or so she had tried to convince herself.

But now the situation had changed. She was here for an indefinite period of time. She'd soon meet friends and neighbors of Jordan—people who would be suspicious about their relationship. She mustn't do anything to fuel that suspicion—not in the community Trevor would grow up in.

Jordan broke the silence first. "Sorry about last night. I shouldn't have done that."

Oh, really? He was right, of course, depending on what he was sorry for. Pretending he'd found her attractive even if he hadn't?

Oh, snap out of it. She'd already convinced herself Jordan had behaved properly. Admit it. Let it go. Today was the first day of the rest of her life—a day in which she'd resolved to be a businesswoman, a nanny, a homemaker, and Jordan Sterling's friend.

Nothing more.

"It's all right." She fixed her gaze firmly on the frying pan. "Guess we were excited because we knew that Trevor really was your son."

"Yes," Jordan said. "And now that we've got that settled, I guess I'd better call my lawyer sooner rather than later. Find out just what our options are, and how we can best protect Trevor."

****

Rosemary had first encountered the erratic weather of Western Alberta in a blinding snowstorm. Now she saw the other side of the coin. A hot dry wind roared over the mountains, making the flowers and grass burst into life, bringing instant summer. The snow disappeared like magic and the thermometer zoomed upwards overnight. The pastures turned green and Jordan stopped his frantic riding of the range. It brought Rosemary a mental lift but increased the restless romantic yearnings of the heart.

Rosemary floated in a suspended land of never-never—a land of a pretend home, a pretend child, a resident cowboy to be part of the pretense. It would end. It must. Then she would face the reality of community, of neighbors, of curiosity, suspicion, and disapproval.

Her fantasy world disintegrated a few days later when Jordan stepped into the kitchen dressed in his good clothes. "Get your jacket. We're going into town. To Wolf River. It isn't very big, but it's close."

"Into town? Now? Both of us? For groceries? You did that yesterday."

"No, not for groceries. I phoned my lawyer, Sidney Perkins. He said he'd look into things for me. I have an appointment with him this afternoon."

"Am I going too?"

"Just to town. Not to the lawyer's office this time. That's no place for Trevor. Maybe you can take him and go to the ladies' store to look at clothes. When I'm finished

54

I'll come across and after that the two of us can do some shopping for Trevor."

"All right." She'd sort of like to meet the lawyer herself, but what Jordan said made sense. "What's he like?"

"He's a good lawyer. Says 'at the moment' so often it drives you crazy, but I guess you don't dump your lawyer because of that."

Chapter Five

Sidney Perkins was middle-aged, plump and balding, wearing glasses that made him look somewhat like an owl. He had been Jordan's lawyer forever, and his parents' lawyer before that. Jordan and he were not quite personal friends, but had a relationship closer than professional. Jordan felt guilty about leaving Rosemary out, but he had the gut feeling that she would be part of the discussion.

He sat down in the chair across the desk from the lawyer, crossed his legs and placed his Stetson on his knee. "So what's the story here?"

"Well," Sidney said, "the story is that Blair, at the moment, holds all the cards. She is the child's biological mother, and, at the moment, as far as I can tell, has broken no laws. Drinking and partying, while undesirable if done to excess, is not illegal. You tell me that she's apparently married to the man of the moment, but, in today's world, even if she weren't, it would not be illegal."

"The plot to sell Trevor?"

Sidney shrugged. "Yes, but, at the moment, you have only Rosemary's unsubstantiated word for that. And, at the moment, Rosemary is a woman who's kidnapped her sister's child."

"But she's cared for Trevor since he was a baby. Blair abandoned him."

"Irrelevant. Face it, Jordan. Blair's holding all the aces and kings. You only have a handful of threes and fours."

"You're telling me it's hopeless?"

"Not totally. But you are starting behind."

"So what do you suggest?"

"A few things. First, give me the address for Rosemary's lawyer in Winnipeg."

"I have it right here." Jordan fumbled in his pocket and handed the lawyer the sheet of paper.

"Good. I'll contact him right away and have him put a private investigator on their trail. If he can get evidence of this selling plot, yes, then you're pretty well home free. Or if he discovers any other criminal activities. Even if he can get evidence that these two would obviously be poor parents, it will help. As far as you know, they have no permanent home. That would also count against them."

"Is there anything further I can do?"

"Yes, there is. You want to have the best home available when they do catch up to you. If Blair comes with the police, I can certainly delay things by telling them about the selling plot. She'll probably be told not to leave Dodge, so to speak, while it's investigated. But in the meantime, you need to work on creating a perfect environment for a child."

Jordan ran his finger down the crown of his hat. "And how do I do that?"

"First, you get married."

"What?" Jordan's hand came down so hard on his Stetson that he crushed it against his leg. "How do you suggest I do that?"

"Well, how about this Rosemary? Maybe you could propose to her."

"I can't marry someone I met only a few days ago." Jordan continued abusing his hat. "Besides, she's a city girl, beautiful and intelligent. I can't ask her to sacrifice herself to a lifetime on this ranch. As I told you on the phone, she's already given up two years of her life for Trevor. I can't ask for more."

The lawyer's lips twitched in a smile. "You're not really that undesirable as husband material yourself, you know. You're young, well off, and handsome. Sure she's never shown any interest in you?"

Jordan grinned self-consciously, and felt a wave of red creep up his neck. He looked at the crown of his mangled hat as he spoke. "She's a young, healthy woman. I suppose she has all the normal urges young healthy women have, but she hasn't done anything about them and probably won't. And neither have I. Anyway, that's not the basis for a marriage. I've had a marriage built on physical desire, and I don't recommend it. Any realistic suggestions for me?"

"Maybe. Sidney tapped the end of his pen on his desk blotter. "Look," he said. "You ever read romance novels?"

Jordan looked startled, but shook his head. "I guess maybe Blair used to."

"Well, I don't either, but Mary does and sometimes she tells me about them. There's something in them called a marriage of convenience. For a practical reason, say an inheritance, a couple get married with the understanding that the marriage will end when it isn't needed anymore. How long they've known each other and how much they have in common is irrelevant. It's a business deal. Now in the stories, of course, the characters fall madly in love and stay married forever, but you and Rosemary wouldn't have to do that."

"So what are you telling me?"

"Just think about it. You and Rosemary get married. Once you have firm custody of Trevor, you can dissolve the marriage. If it isn't consummated, it's a simple matter of an annulment and, in a year or two or whatever it takes, Rosemary can go her way as if she's never been married. You think she'd consider it? I've already filed your application for custody."

"She'll do anything for Trevor." Jordan frowned. "But how soon would we have to get married for that?"

"No rush. In fact, if it were tomorrow, it would look pretty fishy to the family services people. They'd react the same way you did. I'd suggest a few weeks of continuing as you are—spend time getting Rosemary used to the ranch and the community. Then get formally engaged. If Rosemary wants a real wedding, there's still no rush about the ceremony. It would look more authentic given a bit of time. But after the three weeks or so to get acquainted, so to speak, I'd get the diamond on her finger."

"Should she find somewhere else to live?"

Sidney shrugged. "I wouldn't think so. Not in this day and age. Just get that diamond, a nice one, to send the right message. Otherwise, to a judge, she's a liability instead of an asset. Puts the two of you pretty well equal with Blair and what's-his-name. Or below her if they really are married."

"Thanks," Jordan said. "I'll run it by Rosemary.

Anything else?"

"One more thing. I understand you're working that ranch single-handed, not giving you much time to be a father. Hire yourself some help."

Jordan grinned wryly. "Yeah, Rosemary's suggested that too. You're on the same wavelength there."

"Oh, and one last thing." The lawyer stood up and Jordan followed his example. "If this marriage of convenience is going to work, both of you better keep your physical urges under control."

Jordan left the room and walked out onto the street. Sidney Perkins sure had given him enough food for thought.

Rosemary stood near the entrance of the store, Trevor in her arms and a pile of packages around her feet.

"So how'd things go?"

"Let's say I have a lot to think about. We'll talk tonight, after dinner when Trevor's in bed. Right now, let's go shopping for my son."

****

They stowed Rosemary's parcels in the Jeep and walked the few blocks to the hardware store, Rosemary deep in thought. *A lot to think about*, he'd said. *We'll talk tonight*, he'd said.

He hadn't wanted her to go with him to the lawyer. It all smelled like three-day old jackfish under a Winnipeg sun. Was she getting her walking papers? Had the lawyer suggested, in the interests of respectability, of course, that Jordan hire a nice grandmotherly type as a housekeeper?

And between now and tonight's chat, she, Rosemary, was supposed to calmly pick out high chairs and strollers, was she? Just as if this were no more important than the new outfits she'd bought. *Huh!*

"So," Jordan asked when they'd entered the hardware store. "What do we need? A crib?"

"No. Not a crib. He's doing just fine on the bottom bunk. If we put him in a crib, in less than a year we'd have to put him in a different bed anyway." *Less than a year*. She paused. Where would all of them be in another year?

Jordan would be here, of course. Hopefully, Trevor would still be here too. Unless Blair found out where he

59

was, and managed to get her hands on him.

Rosemary herself? She'd probably be back in Winnipeg, unless she'd disappeared with Trevor to Peace River or Regina or Outer Mongolia to keep one step ahead of Blair and the law. She suspected that tonight's mysterious talk meant she'd leave here sooner rather than later.

She dragged her attention back to shopping. "Maybe one of those play-pens that folds up like a suitcase. It can double as a crib if he has to sleep away from home."

"Fine. What else?"

"How about a high-chair? Sure make feeding him easier. And a stroller, so I don't have to walk at his speed or tuck him under my arm."

A young clerk walked briskly down the aisle, rubbing his hands together hopefully. "Hi, Mr. Sterling." Curiosity oozed out his ears. "Something for you? Visitors?" He glanced at Trevor perched on Jordan's arm and at Rosemary.

The two women at the check-out counter quit counting their supply of plastic bags and listened.

"My son," Jordan told them proudly. "This is my son, Trevor."

One of the check-out women, the one with the pointed nose, left her post and casually sauntered down to the furniture department. "Oh, so sweet." She patted Trevor's shoulder. He smiled at her and made gooey noises.

"He's just so sweet, Jordan. I didn't know you had a son."

"Neither did I, until a few days ago."

The woman looked from Jordan to Rosemary.

"This, um, is my sister-in-law." Jordan cleared his throat. "Leila Simpson. Rosemary Robbins."

The woman continued to smile, but her gaze sharpened. "Oh. I see. The baby was with your brother's family when he was small?"

Rosemary stepped forward and held out her hand. She smiled too. She could do fake smiles with the best of them. Leila shook her hand.

"No," Rosemary said. "I'm Blair's sister. You know. Blair was Jordan's ex-wife. I've been keeping the baby.

But Blair has gone her own way, and I thought it only right that Jordan should get to know his son."

"I see." Leila looked shrewdly at Jordan.

Jordan ignored the speculative gaze and turned to the young clerk. "We'll take this high chair, if you'd just box it up. And that playpen." He pointed again. "And that stroller."

"Yes, sir."

Leila stayed where she was. There were no customers needing attention at the check-out counter.

"Anything else, sir?" the clerk asked.

"I think we'll check out the toy department," Jordan said. Before long, a heap of toys was piled on the floor: a model farm, complete with barn and house and corrals and horses and cows and sheep, and two farm dogs that just happened to look a lot like Ben and Buster; a mobile of dolphins to hang from the bottom of the upper bunk where Trevor could bat at it; and a variety of balls and building blocks.

Trevor had been quite happy to play with pots and pans, but obviously Jordan wanted to buy toys for him.

Leila still stood at the back of the store. She turned to Rosemary. "So you'll be visiting at the Sterling ranch for awhile?"

"Yes." *Maybe.* Rosemary's face ached from smiling. "I'm helping Mr. Sterling take care of Trevor for now."

"I see." The woman strolled back slowly to her counter.

Rosemary seethed inwardly. Easy to see what the woman thought. In two hours it would be all over town. The nerve of her, smiling steadily from both her faces while she longed for the end of the day so she could phone everybody she knew with the dirt on Jordan Sterling and his sister-in-law.

Rosemary could hear her now. *If she even is his sister-in-law. Sure doesn't look anything like his wife.* Well, there was nothing Rosemary could do about it. Nothing at all. If she protested that she was nothing but sister-in-law and nanny to Jordan Sterling, she'd only add fuel to the fire.

At the next stop, a general store, she bought a variety of tops and overalls for Trevor.

"Look here. Isn't this cool?" Jordan pointed to an outfit hanging on the wall—toddler sized jeans, western shirt and cream-colored Stetson.

"It's darling," Rosemary agreed.

Jordan bought the outfit. He also introduced Rosemary to the clerks in the children's department. Both shook her hand with great affability, but when the bill was paid and the clothes in plastic bags, Rosemary saw the look that passed between the two women as she and Jordan and Trevor went out the door.

Something had to be done about this, but at the moment Rosemary wasn't sure what. She'd have to think about it. If Jordan told her to pack her bags tomorrow, none of it would matter. In any case, there was no point in discussing it with Jordan. He wouldn't know what she was talking about. He'd just look at her in surprise and say something profound like, *Well, they seemed very friendly to me.*

****

While Jordan bathed Trevor and got him ready for bed, Rosemary wallowed in a prolonged bath, piled high with bubbles and smelling of roses. Okay. So she'd indulged in overkill. She didn't know what this momentous discussion Jordan had suggested was all about. Something coming out of his interview with the lawyer.

Did the lawyer think she shouldn't be here? Did Jordan want her to leave? If that was it, she'd show him she wouldn't miss him. Show him she was a beautiful sensuous woman of the new millennium who didn't need him or any other man. Rosemary Robbins would make out just fine, thank you. Without Jordan, without the ranch. Without Trevor?

If that's what he wanted to talk about.

She scurried from the tub and grabbed a towel.

As she dried herself off in front of the mirror, she took inventory. Good body. Trim waist. Tight hips. Full firm breasts. A body that, upon at least one occasion, Jordan Sterling had fancied.

Forget it. A daydream. The thing to do was to hang on to her self-respect and go with class. A woman of the twenty-first century. Confident and self-sufficient.

She brushed her hair until it gleamed, then put on her robe and walked back to the computer room. The clothes she intended to wear for their little chat were laid out, waiting for her. She'd put them there earlier to avoid encountering Jordan when he put Trevor to bed. That's all she'd need—another lust-driven confrontation before they even started talking.

She dressed carefully in an emerald shirt of soft silk that clung and shimmered and matched her eyes. With it she wore green linen pants. She buttoned up the shirt and zipped the pants, then tightened the self-belt that made her waist seem smaller and her breasts and hips swell out above and below it.

The mirrored closet door reflected back her image. She looked good. She peered at herself and shook her head. Too formal. She unbuttoned the cuffs of the shirt and flipped them back, exposing her wrists and lower forearms. She dabbed perfume that smelled like wild flowers on each wrist. Take that, Jordan Sterling.

When she walked into the family room, he was seated in his leather recliner, feet propped on the raised footrest, head leaned against the back.

The heart of the millennium woman pounded in her chest.

Jordan stood, and waved her to the other easy chair.

"Sit down, Rosemary." He acted as stiff and formal as the queen's butler.

Obviously *he* didn't have emotions raging out of control. But then, *he* wasn't losing Trevor and the ranch. If that's what he wanted to talk about.

"I'll pour coffee for us," he said, "and then we'll discuss what we're going to do. By the way, you look good tonight."

So I look good, do I, Jordan Sterling? Just by the way, of course.

She sat down, legs tucked under her, hands arranged casually in her lap, the tips of her fingers crushed between her thighs to prevent their trembling.

Jordan returned so fast Rosemary knew he'd had the coffee waiting. She grasped the proffered mug in both hands, looking at Jordan over the top of it, memorizing more pictures for the album of her soul. The silence spun out. They sipped coffee and stalled, each waiting for the other to make the initial move.

"You want me to leave? Is that it?" The stiff upper lip quivered and the self-respect drained out through her toes and disappeared beneath the floor, beneath the floor joists, and beneath the cement floor of the basement.

Jordan jerked up his head and pierced her heart with his bright blue eyes. He looked at her—was it speculatively? Did he suspect how she felt? She pressed one hand against her not-so-stiff upper lip and babbled through her fingers.

"I can't give up Trevor. Please. Please, let me stay." Her tears ran down the edges of her nose, collected against the finger which pressed her lip into her teeth, then dripped onto the shining silk of her green shirt, leaving fat wet blobs.

Jordan stared at her, speechless.

Tears streamed down her face faster than she could mop them up. The tissue in her hand disintegrated, scattering particles of wet shredded paper everywhere. She looked around helplessly.

"Here." Jordan stood, searched his own pockets without luck, then unbuttoned his shirt and took it off. He knelt before her and wiped her face on the warm flannel. Rosemary's mouth went dry. She'd never seen him less than fully clothed. *This* was supposed to help, this vision of Jordan Sterling half-naked—his broad shoulders, sculpted muscles, the dark hair on his chest narrowing to a vee as it disappeared into the top of his jeans and on down... The shirt against her face was warm with his body heat, and the smell of him lingered in it.

How could she? In the sorrow of losing Trevor, how could she possibly be sidetracked into thinking about sex? She began to hiccup.

"Oh, hell. Rosemary, honey. What do you want me to do?"

"Let me stay. Please. Just let me stay. I'll vacuum and scrub and bake pies for you, and..."

Her words disappeared in a round of louder hiccups. She stood up abruptly and brushed past Jordan. She picked Trevor's forsaken teddy bear from the playpen and crushed it to her breasts, then stood looking blindly into the dark window.

She saw Jordan, still hunkered down, reflected in the window glass. Savagely, she yanked the drapes closed, bit her lower lip so hard she tasted blood, and turned to face him.

He stood up, holding the tear-stained shirt. "Settle down, Rosemary. I'm not sending you away."

"No?"

"No. I'm trying to ask you to marry me."

"Marry you?" The blood drained from Rosemary's face. "You want me to marry you?"

Jordan stared at the woodstove. "Yes."

A proposal of marriage from Jordan Sterling? The thought of being in bed with Jordan Sterling boosted her pulse rate. As did the thought of sitting across from him at the dinner table for the rest of her life. Gazing at the mountains with him for the rest of her life.

Had she subconsciously had a proposal in the back of her mind when she bathed, lingering in the scented bubble bath, then dressing carefully in the green silk shirt? That imagined proposal, the hope she'd refused to acknowledge to herself, had featured him throwing himself on her mercy, asking her to marry him because neither he nor Trevor could live without her.

But now he'd proposed with a remarkable lack of enthusiasm, unable to look at her, forcing out the words as if being drawn and quartered would have been a more desirable fate. All of this because he felt sorry for her? Or because he needed a wife and she was handy? Could she accept a marriage based on pity, or self-interest, even for Trevor?

The bottom line was, yes, she could. If she could accept it, nobody in the community would ever know what this marriage really was—a bone thrown to her from compassion, as if to a starving dog.

"That's why I asked for this meeting. So I could propose."

"Then what took you so long?"

"I had to get you settled down first, get you to stop crying. Now just be quiet while I explain. I don't want you to say anything until you hear me out. Sidney Perkins suggested something that he referred to as a marriage of convenience. I know that a real marriage between us wouldn't be a good idea. But would you consider that? A marriage of convenience for Trevor's sake?"

Her heart plummeted. It was like being told you'd won the lottery and then being handed a cupful of ashes. But she would not start crying again. She absolutely would not. After all, a woman had to have her pride.

And then there was Trevor.

A marriage of convenience? Because the lawyer had suggested it? Was there no limit to what she'd do for Trevor? Apparently not. She stepped toward Jordan, head high, the teddy bear a buffer. "Yes." She nodded. "If you're sure, I'll marry you. For Trevor."

"All right. Why don't you sit down? I'll get fresh coffee, and we'll talk about it."

Talk about it? What was there to say? Not *I love you.* Not *I can't live without you.* But *will you marry me because my lawyer feels it would be a good idea*?

She sipped her coffee, looked at Jordan through her lashes, and waited. Her pride told her to refuse. But she couldn't leave Trevor.

Well, he could say whatever had to be said next. She'd made a big enough fool of herself for one evening. If Jordan could handle a marriage with the same composure he'd use to buy a horse, fine. Let him just go ahead.

Finally he spoke. "So my lawyer suggested that we get married. I know that you wouldn't want to marry me, and I don't want to marry anybody, but I guess I have to. With what he described, we can do this without ruining the rest of your life. We'll stay married until I have full custody of Trevor. Then I can let you go. If the marriage isn't consummated, it can be dissolved as a simple annulment, and after it's over, you'll be the same as an unmarried woman again."

She shut her eyes and shuddered. Was there no end to her humiliation? He spoke the words as dispassionately as if he'd memorized a written script Sidney Perkins had given him.

Which was probably the case.

"I see." Rosemary crossed her hands in front of her throat as if he could see the knives she swallowed in her hurt. "A fast trip to the justice of the peace at the beginning and another at the end. That's what you're saying. Starting tomorrow, I suppose."

"No. Sidney said that would look too suspicious to the family services people. We go on as we are. Then when two or three weeks have passed, enough time for people to think we've fallen in love, we'll announce our engagement. Sidney said if you wanted a real wedding, a diamond on your finger will do as well while a real wedding gets organized."

"I see." Rosemary felt as icy as her words sounded. "I certainly wouldn't want to do anything that Sidney wouldn't approve of."

"Look." Jordan ran one hand through his hair. "It was just an idea he had. If you find it that distasteful, we can forget the whole thing. You go back to Winnipeg and I'll start attending a church with a young adults' social group that's eighty percent women desperately looking for a husband."

"Huh. I said I'd do it, and I'll do it. For Trevor."

"Of course. For Trevor."

"I suppose I'll have to sign a paper like Blair did, saying that I won't get any of your cows or oil wells?" Not that she cared about that in the slightest.

"I'm sure that Sidney will draw up something that's fair to everyone concerned."

She lifted her coffee. Instead of throwing the whole thing in his face as she wanted to do, she sipped it and took a deep breath to steady herself. "All right. What happens next and when?"

"Nothing much for a couple of weeks."

"Huh." She was stung by his practical approach to what should be emotional and sentimental. "And am I supposed to live in a motel in the meantime?"

He paused. "No. Sidney said that in this day and age that shouldn't be necessary."

The hair on Rosemary's neck prickled with suppressed anger. The man hadn't even recognized her sarcasm. He'd thought she really was offering to move out.

"I'm sorry I asked you so abruptly. I'd intended to discuss everything calmly. But then you got on a roll and couldn't stop crying, and I couldn't get a word in. That's why I asked you so suddenly."

"I—I—I..." She still could think of nothing to say. This was getting worse and worse.

Jordan continued. "Sidney's also going to get in touch with your lawyer, and encourage him to find a private investigator in the area. I gave him the number and address."

Rosemary jumped to her feet, clenched her fists and jammed them into her pockets. "Is there anything else?"

"Not really. Finish your coffee and I'll fill you in on the background."

"Yes. Why don't you do that?" She remained standing and left the coffee mug where it was.

"Well, apparently as things stand now, Blair has the law on her side. Hopefully the PI will find evidence of something illegal. The fact that they don't have a permanent home will go against them too. But he wasn't too impressed with my home either—a bachelor, running a large ranch single-handed. Therefore, I have to be in the process of establishing a very suitable home. You'll be happy to hear that this suitable home includes a hired man so that I can spend more time with Trevor."

"Well." Rosemary fought to keep her voice from trembling. "I'm glad that one thing is turning out right." She knew that her face gave her away.

"Look at it this way. It's a job. Just a continuation of what you're doing now. I'll pay you."

"I don't want your wretched money."

"But you'll do it?"

"I said I would."

He continued. "Now, what kind of wedding do we want?"

"Simple. I don't think we need a lot of fuss. I guess we'll both want a small wedding."

"All right. Whatever you say." He looked away from her. She examined his jaw line—firm and straight. Then he turned to face her, his blue eyes boring into hers. "Listen, I'll marry you. I know you love Trevor and he loves you. But you have to understand there's one thing I can't give you. I can't give you love."

She glared at him. "I know. You've made that quite obvious."

She flushed at his glance.

"I don't love you. I know you don't love me. I won't bother you. I'll keep my end of the bargain to not consummate the marriage to make things easier for you." He stood abruptly and leaned toward her, holding the back of his chair to brace himself. "I'll put up a good front for the neighbors. And for Trevor. I'll try never to embarrass or humiliate you. As the lawyer said, it's a marriage of convenience. I'll make it as convenient for you as I can. Can you accept that?"

Don't do me any favors. She couldn't say it aloud. This proposal was her only chance to stay with Trevor, and to do her best to keep Trevor safe. Her only other choice was to leave. Without Trevor.

"Yes." Her back was rigid and her voice steady. "I accept it. Because I don't love you either. I could never live with a man if I loved him but he didn't love me. Or the other way around."

What a lot of garbage they both spouted. But why not? Wasn't that how people arranged business contracts? This was just another business contract like the ones she signed with her clients.

Jordan cleared his throat. "I know you love Trevor like he was your own. I'll make sure you still get to spend time with him after the annulment."

She supposed she should be happy. After all, she'd gotten what she wanted. Jordan had agreed to marry her, because he felt sorry for her and because he needed a wife. He was also scrupulously truthful. Trevor was still hers and would be forever, at least part time.

Just the same, she wished her marriage was going to be based on more than pity and convenience and the advice of a lawyer. She wished the groom would at least pretend he'd like to be married to her forever.

Chapter Six

"I think it's time we started giving and going to social events," Rosemary announced over breakfast the next morning.

Jordan spooned scrambled eggs into Trevor's open mouth, then put down the spoon. "What do you mean?"

"Just what I said. I think the idea was that we were getting acquainted so an engagement would be more believable. Well, what's the point in getting acquainted if nobody notices?"

Jordan raised his eyebrows.

Rosemary soldiered on. "I've been here for a week and a half now, but so far no one else has come to the ranch, and if anyone has invited you anywhere, I'm not aware of it. I haven't met a soul here other than store clerks." *And they've given both of us some mighty funny looks.* Not that Jordan would have noticed. Men wore blinders when it came to things like that.

Jordan inclined his head toward Trevor. "Do you really think this is the place and time to discuss it?"

"Yes. I chose this time. Trevor isn't old enough to know what we're talking about if we keep our voices friendly and cheerful. He would be upset if we were fighting. This way, there's no chance of a discussion becoming a fight."

"I see." Not raising his voice, he added, "You mean, you're like Blair. You hanker for the bright lights?"

"No." Rosemary smiled sweetly if not sincerely. "I'm not like Blair. Blair wanted parties with the fast crowd she met at the Calgary Stampede. I'm quite happy to get to know the women on neighboring ranches. And if we're working up to this marriage, it's a necessity." Her voice dripped saccharine. "I'm sure the social workers will be much more impressed with a wife who takes part in community life than they would with a hermit."

She got up, and reached for the coffeepot to refill

their cups.

"Just tell me. How long is it since you've had a barbecue and invited some of your neighbors?"

Trevor reached his arms out and made a greedy noise, like a baby bird licking its chops if baby birds did that. Jordan returned to his duties with the eggs.

Taking time to think, was he? Stalling, was he? Well, let him.

Eggs gone, Jordan looked at her. "Well, I don't know. Quite a while, I guess. I guess maybe before Mom and Dad were killed."

"Which was?"

"Five years ago. I didn't have much heart for it for awhile. And then I met Blair and got married. I think maybe I did that because I wanted a family again. But Blair wasn't, as she put it, into sitting around with a bunch of dull farm wives, discussing casserole recipes and potty training."

"Five years is a long time to be a hermit, Jordan. I think it's time to face the world. For Trevor, if not for yourself."

She watched his jaw muscle tighten. Good thing she'd chosen the ground for this consultation wisely. Otherwise they'd be having a flaming row by now and the issue never would be settled.

"What about you?"

"What about me?"

"Aren't people going to talk? You living here with me like this."

She'd sure been right about men being clueless. What did he think all the undercurrents in the hardware store had been about? That was a no-brainer. He hadn't even noticed there'd been any.

She had an urge to laugh hysterically, but instead she laid her fork across the edge of her plate and leaned forward, elbows on the table, chin just above her clasped hands. "Jordan, trust me. People are talking right now. Jordan Sterling, the man with the flaky wife. She's gone away, you know. Can't say as I blame her. He never set foot outside his ranch after she left. And now he has some *woman* there. They were together in the hardware store. Buying baby things. Bold as brass. Her sister's baby.

Huh!"

Rosemary saw a dull flush of red on Jordan's cheekbones.

She pressed her advantage. "It appears I'm in this for the long haul. And even if I weren't, you'd still be here. You and Trevor. Because your reputation will haunt him. One flake and one floozy. Don't you think it's time to stop hiding as if we're guilty of something? Don't you realize that we have to establish ourselves as friends—brother and sister-in-law, then as an engaged couple, and finally as man and wife? And the whole thing has to look realistic."

Trevor, breakfast finished, followed the conversation with his head, like a spectator at a tennis match.

"All right. So we're going to face all the neighbors, are we? And you've worked out exactly what you're going to tell them?"

"Yes, the truth." She'd been awake half the night working out what she was going to tell them, working out her strategy. She didn't intend to share all of that with Jordan Sterling. It would go right over his head anyway. "Well, part of the truth. Blair left. She had a baby. Then she decided to remarry and the new man didn't want children, so she left Trevor with me, and asked me to return him to you. I've returned him. But at the moment, you're in no position to care for him yourself, so I agreed to stay. I have a consulting service, so I can work any place where I can plug in my computer."

She chuckled. "Who knows? Maybe I'll even pick up a few more customers." She added, "I won't tell them about the plot to sell Trevor, and I won't badmouth Blair, no more than the facts imply. If they ask why she left, I'll tell the truth there too. She was a city woman, and she couldn't stand the lonely life of a rancher's wife."

"You think that will stop gossip?"

She spread her hands and shrugged. "I don't know. But I do know the chances are a lot better than hiding out here with everybody speculating about who I am, who Trevor is, how you met me, and why I buy your groceries." *Why everyone I see here, including the check-out woman in the hardware store, looks at us with suspicion in their eyes.*

72

Jordan drained his coffee cup and avoided looking at her.

"Besides, I think we both need a wider range of friendships. If it were winter and we lived up north, it would be called cabin fever. People with cabin fever do strange things."

"All right. You've made your point." He tore tiny pieces off a muffin and began hand-feeding them to Trevor. "In fact, when I went to the post office yesterday, Len Peterson said they were having a barbecue Saturday and suggested we come. I didn't commit myself. I figured they asked me out of curiosity and that they could drown in it. Peterson's is the second ranch to the west."

Rosemary smiled. "Wonderful. Perfect, in fact. Could you phone him and tell him we'll be there? And find out things like whether I should bring a salad or dessert, what time we're expected, and what the dress code is if you don't already know."

He gave her a small, mocking bow. "Your wish is my command. They'll say you don't have to bring anything, but I know they'll appreciate it if you do. And the dress code is jeans and a shirt."

"Excellent." She took a damp cloth and wiped the tray of Trevor's high chair.

Jordan disappeared down the hall with the child to change his diaper and dress him.

"Excellent," she murmured again, to herself this time.

She cleaned the kitchen with brisk efficiency and began to make her plans. Her chocolate cheesecake was to die for. She'd go to town this afternoon and get the ingredients and a springform pan. The cake would be an icebreaker. A great dessert always was. Women clamored for the recipe.

She'd wear her newest Levi's with a shirt of cream-colored suede silk and a scarf colored like a rainbow with tiny gold threads running through it. She'd bought those items just last week and hadn't yet worn them.

She'd wow them. She'd win them. She'd let the world know what really went on at the Sterling ranch. And what didn't.

Jordan Sterling's live-in floozy?

Not bloody likely!

****

Rosemary phoned her parents to bring them up to date on events—that Jordan had accepted Trevor, that she would remain on at the ranch for awhile, that no one must know where she was. And would her mother mind checking the apartment? And arrange for a cleaning service? She could not yet share the information that her absence would be semi-permanent and she had no further use for the apartment. That announcement would come in a couple more weeks.

A few days later, while she bathed Trevor, Rosemary taught him to say *Daddy*. It was time. *That* would probably impress the lawyer and social workers too. "Daddy," she told him as he splashed bath water about. "Say *Daddy*."

"Da," Trevor repeated.

"Da-Da," Rosemary said. "Say *Da-Da*. Da-Da."

"Da-Da."

"Now *Dee*. Say *Dee*."

"Dee. Dee. Dee. Dee." He thumped his hand against the surface of the water and sprayed Rosemary's shirt.

She laughed and kissed the top of his head. "Good. Good. Now, *Da-Dee. Da-Dee*."

"Da-Dee, Da-Dee, Da-Dee, Da-Dee—" He put a rhythm to it and turned it into a chant.

"Okay, friend. Well done." She picked Trevor up, laid him on a bath towel and tickled his tummy. "What do you say? Again. Da-Dee."

"Da-Dee, Da-Dee, Da-Dee—"

Whenever Trevor learned a new word, he babbled it, again and again and again. Rosemary dried him to the accompaniment of the non-stop chant. At least, he'd still remember the word when Jordan came in for lunch.

She dressed him in the cute little jeans and red checked shirt Jordan had bought, then tied a red bandanna around his neck and parked his miniature Stetson on his head. They went out to the deck. Trevor played with his collection of plastic stacking toys, and Rosemary settled herself in the old-fashioned porch swing to read. The two yellow farm dogs came up to sniff at her and Trevor, than wandered back out into the yard.

Rosemary's book lay forgotten as she gazed at the panorama before her. The barns and corrals were to the side of the house. In front, the driveway ran past a couple of unoccupied bungalows. Someday she'd have to ask Jordan about those. Beyond the bungalows, green pastures dotted with red cattle stretched to the road. At one side, a small creek rambled between rows of trees. There were probably wild spring flowers too, but from here she couldn't see them. The Rockies formed a backdrop for the whole thing.

Yes, she should pound out ideas for her clients on the computer. Yes, she should vacuum the carpets and run the mop over the kitchen floor. Yes, she should start lunch. But on a day like this, who cared? She'd work at the computer when Trevor was in bed. The house could stay dirty. Jordan would play with Trevor while she got lunch.

Meanwhile, she'd sit in the sun and read and dream. She gazed at the white and purple mountains and wove fantasies about them and the clouds above them. She knew they were just piles of rocks and ice, but that's not what they looked like from here. The ancient Greeks thought their gods lived in a place much like that. Maybe they did. She felt right now that she could fly off to the distant peaks, and land in Heaven without going through the usual unpleasantness prerequisite to getting there.

She breathed deeply of the sweet, warm air. Maybe she was already in Heaven. At least when she could forget, for the moment, the blasted marriage of convenience which faced her.

The farm truck swung into the driveway, and Rosemary lifted Trevor in her arms, ready to meet Jordan. Ben and Buster romped ahead of her. Jordan slammed the door of the pickup and ran up the walk.

He held out his arms. "Daddy's little cowboy."

Rosemary whispered into Trevor's ear. "Say *Da-Dee*. Say *Da-Dee*."

"Da-Dee, Da-Dee, Da-Dee." Trevor roared the words. He bounced against Rosemary in his rush to go to Jordan. A horrid little shaft of jealousy shot through her. Neither of them needed her. Nobody needed her. After Jordon had custody firmly nailed down, she'd return to her spinster apartment in Winnipeg and neither of them would ever think of her again.

She swallowed her petty lump of bitterness and smiled. She held Trevor out so that Jordan could take him from her.

He grinned. "He called me *Daddy*. You heard him?"

"Yes. I heard him."

She tried to say the words without emotion, tried to harden her heart, but she couldn't. Not when she looked at the love on Jordan's face when Trevor called him *Daddy*. It had been worth it all. The time putting up with Blair, the fear that had lodged in her throat like splintered bones, the long drive west, Jordan's suspicions and his open distrust. It had been worth every hour of it to see this one moment of pure joy on Jordan's face.

At that moment she could have loved Jordan Sterling.

Not that he'd have cared. The nasty bitter nugget of jealousy returned. None of the joy was for her. She could have been sixty-five with twelve grandchildren for all Jordan cared. Except that a sixty-five year old bride probably wouldn't make the right impression.

She slipped into the house to make lunch. She doubted they even noticed she was missing.

After lunch, Jordan put Trevor down for his nap. Rosemary had finished cleaning up by time he came back.

"Let's sit in the swing for a while?"

She followed him out the front door and eased into the swing, keeping firmly to her own side. Jordan sat relaxed, one booted foot propped on the knee of the other leg, his black Stetson resting on his bent knee. She blinked her eyes and swallowed. She couldn't bear this, being so close, trying to convince herself she didn't care.

"Look." He turned toward her. "I owe you an apology. Truth is, you're an angel sent from Heaven, coming with the little guy, giving me the son I've dreamed of having. You've taken care of both of us, in spite of all the grief I've given you."

"No problem." Rosemary tried to put the sexy jeans and black Stetson from her mind and swallowed the lump of bitterness that had lodged itself in her throat. "For a few minutes there, before you dropped the information about her so-called sterility, you almost had me thinking you hadn't been sleeping together or something." She grinned wryly. "Guess you were." The very thought of it shot pain through her heart, much as she told herself she didn't care.

"Yeah, we were. If the rest of our marriage had been as good as the sex, there'd have been no problem."

The pain in her heart struck again.

He continued, "Blair was very, uh, good in bed, I guess you call it. Very experienced. Hell of a lot more experienced than I was. It took me a while to figure that part of it out. But I took my marriage vows seriously, and planned to stick it out for the rest of my life. Even when the sex didn't appeal much toward the end, after I'd fallen out of love, we still slept together until she left. Even if kids weren't on her agenda."

Rosemary reached toward him impulsively, then jerked back, remembering his promise to keep their relationship platonic, her own resolution to stick to friendship. Remembering that she had to get used to the idea of a sexless marriage.

He hesitated. "The whole marriage was a mistake," he said finally. "She saw me as glamorous. We met at an after-stampede party. I wore my dressiest movie-star-cowboy shirt. We danced and talked. She flirted with me. Pursued me. The bottom line was she wanted my body and my wallet. I think she'd have been happy with a brief affair, but I was naive enough to confuse sexual desire with love."

His laugh was bitter. "She visualized life on the ranch as a Western soap opera where she could dress in expensive clothes and entertain expensive friends. We discovered our mistake before the honeymoon ended." He pinched the crown of his hat. "But I still don't understand. Why did she wait until she was pregnant to leave?"

"I think she wanted out. She told me you wanted a baby so badly that if you'd known she was pregnant you'd have found some way to keep her for the rest of her life, tied down with a baby. Then she sponged off me for nearly two years. What could I do? I loved Trevor, and couldn't do anything that might end up hurting him. I was relieved when she found a new man and left. Until I realized what the new man was like." A shiver struck her at the memory of that overheard conversation.

"I guess I know what you mean. I was sure relieved when she divorced me, no matter where she went to do it."

"Why didn't you divorce her?"

He shrugged. "No point. I had no intention of remarrying. I was just glad to be rid of her."

Good reminder. Just in case she had any ideas that this might turn into a real marriage.

Jordan looked at Rosemary long and hard. "You did the right thing bringing Trevor here. And again, agreeing to this marriage to protect his future. Trevor will be safe. I promise you that. And I promise to release you the moment that safety is assured."

Rosemary froze, then stuck out one foot and put the swing in motion, trying to look nonchalant. "You know, at some point, I'd have brought him here anyway. Even if I'd eventually been able to get custody, I'd never have felt totally secure. Blair's unpredictable. She might convince a judge she's mother of the year and deserves her child back. She can be very charming when she wants to. But I know that she could never become a fit mother."

"You think I'm a fit father?"

She grinned at him. "Would I have taught him to call you Daddy otherwise?"

He stretched out one arm to place it behind her shoulders, then jerked it back and clasped his knee. "I'll sort all this out as soon as I can. I know it's not fun here for a young woman. Blair sure told me that often enough."

"It's beautiful. The house, the ranch, the mountains. I love it." Well, she told herself, she did love all those things. "I promise, I'll stay and run the business from here until our lawyers have ensured that Trevor will be safe."

She cleared her throat. "Uh, speaking of lawyers—I don't suppose you've heard anything more yet. About the private investigator and things? After all, it's been only a couple of days."

"As a matter of fact," Jordan said, "I did."

"So what did he say?"

"Your lawyer told him there wasn't any immediate panic. I guess he knows your parents too and contacted them first."

"Yes, he does. He's sort of the family lawyer. And a personal friend of my dad. So have Mom and Dad heard anything?"

"Yeah. Apparently, Blair's first place to look was up around where your parents live. She did the prodigal daughter thing. Wanted to mend fences with her parents. Then she wanted to mend fences with Rosemary too, but didn't know where to find her."

He chuckled. "Your mother must have been an actress in a former life. She told Blair she had no idea where you were, but projected body language that said she was lying. So Blair and her man—"

"Roscoe," Rosemary prompted. "His name's Roscoe."

"Yeah, that's right. Anyway Blair and Roscoe have booked into a local motel for a couple of weeks so they can watch the comings and goings at your parents' house. Your lawyer said they fancy themselves really good at the spy stuff, but they're so obvious it's laughable."

"The only thing Roscoe's good at is drinking. Anything else?"

"Not really. So we now have a sleuth dogging their steps while they play at sleuthing your parents." He shrugged. "Sidney was delighted to hear that you'd agreed to the marriage he suggested."

Bully for Sidney.

****

"Come on," Jordan said to Rosemary after breakfast the following day. "I'll get the little guy ready while you stack the dishwasher, and then we're going riding."

Sidney Perkins had suggested that the time before the formal engagement be spent getting Rosemary used to ranch life.

Rosemary looked doubtful

"Hey. Turn about's fair play. I agreed to introduce you to the social life of the community, so now it's your turn to humor me by learning how to ride."

Her reaction wasn't great. "Riding?" she said. "Like on a horse? Huh-uh. I love the ranch. But riding? The closest I've ever been to a horse is watching the races at Assiniboine Downs." She looked as wild-eyed and panicked as a roped maverick. "I've never been on a horse except for the day you rescued me from the storm."

Jordan chuckled and bounced Trevor in his arms. She wasn't getting out of it that easily.

"What about Trevor?"

"Trevor will ride with me. And I'll get you a horse so fat and lazy you won't know you're moving."

She shrugged. "All right. If you insist. What do I wear?"

"It's a nice day. Just what you're wearing. Put on boots and a light jacket."

His glance moved over her snug jeans and flannel shirt and watched the swing of her hips as she walked down the hall to her room. Maybe this wasn't such a great idea. He'd better control himself and take it slow and easy.

By time she returned, Jordan and Trevor were ready. He swung the child into the air and caught him.

"Hossy. Hossy. Hossy."

"That's right, little guy." He placed Trevor on his shoulders and held his feet to secure him. "Ride a horsy. Just like this." He bent his knees going through the door, then jogged, bouncing Trevor up and down.

Rosemary came with them from the house, glancing at him and smiling tensely, almost as if she sensed what he was thinking. Nobody looked that nervous about getting on a horse.

"Here, you hold Trevor while I get Molly and Satan."

Rosemary caught the child and pulled him to her.

Jordan ducked back into the barn and returned with Satan and a plump white mare. "This is Molly." He pointed to the white horse. "I've had her forever. Fat and gentle and lazy."

Rosemary put out a trembling hand to stroke the mare's nose. Trevor grabbed an ear and pulled it. "Hossy. Hossy."

Molly stood placidly while Jordan parked Trevor on a hay bale and helped Rosemary mount. He cupped one hand over her boot and guided it into the stirrup. When he demonstrated how to use the reins, his hand brushed hers accidentally, sending a jolt of electricity through him. She snatched her hand away.

So she felt it too, though she obviously hadn't wanted

to.

Jordan tucked his hands into the front pockets of his jeans while Rosemary fiddled with the reins. Molly stood stone still, switching her tail.

Finally, Jordan led Satan through the gate. Molly followed while Rosemary sat stiff. Jordan plunked Trevor into Satan's saddle and swung up behind him. He clucked to his horse. "Giddyup, Satan."

The horses walked side by side. "Giddyup, giddyup, giddyup," Trevor chanted,

Jordan watched Rosemary's body adjust to the rhythm of the horse. Eventually she actually smiled, and her body relaxed as she swayed with the motion. She looked as if she enjoyed the rolling vistas of new grass, the fresh springtime greens of the birch and poplar leaves, the Rockies looming ahead of them.

"It's beautiful." She inhaled great gulps of warm air. "The wild roses are everywhere. Their perfume makes the world smell sweet." She breathed deeply.

"Yes. They're Alberta's official flower—the wild rose."

The wind ruffled Molly's mane and caressed Rosemary's hair. "Heaven." She stroked the side of the horse's neck. "It's absolute Heaven."

Jordan thought so too. The wild roses covered every road ditch, the sides of every cow path, every fence line. And Rosemary was right. Their perfume made the whole world sweet.

He watched her. She looked like a cowgirl in a western movie, riding with the cowboy hero and their child.

In his dreams.

They rode on. Clumps of white-faced cattle spotted the grassland. They looked plump and contented. They apparently hadn't suffered from the recent blizzard. His working day and night had kept them safe. He'd work even harder to keep Trevor safe. Even if that included marriage.

****

"Hi!" On Saturday afternoon, Rosemary stepped into the kitchen of the Peterson ranch house, cheesecake in hand, and faced the most likely candidate for hostess. Jordan and Trevor were outside around the barbecue or the horseshoe pits or wherever. She imagined it was the typical farm community party—women in one place, men in the other, until the food was dished up.

"Where should I put this?" Rosemary asked, holding out the cheesecake.

The woman smiled and took it. "Oooh. That looks good." She opened the fridge door, and found a space for the cheesecake.

"Actually, it is. Very good." Rosemary extended her hand. "I'm Rosemary Robbins. I guess you'd say I'm Jordan Sterling's sister-in-law. Blair is my older sister, by a couple of years."

"Pleased to meet you." The woman who owned the fridge shook Rosemary's hand. "I'm Lois Peterson. Sorry I never met your sister." Lois was pert and dark, probably about ten years older than Rosemary.

"I know," Rosemary kept her voice bright and cheerful. "Poor Blair. She just wasn't cut out for ranch life. Not cut out for motherhood either, I guess. You have any kids?"

Lois introduced all the other women in the room. As the conversation rolled on, Rosemary slid in the information she wanted to get across, all the things she'd told Jordan she intended to give out and a bit more. Lois hung on her every word. The circle of women listened eagerly.

Good. The more the merrier. The fewer times she had to repeat it, the less chance there was of someone else getting it all wrong as the story passed from person to person. The more chance that somebody would say to another person, *You know. That woman at the Sterling ranch. She really is Jordan's sister-in-law. She told me that herself, and you know something, I believe her.*

She said nothing about the fact that Jordan and she weren't sleeping together. That could sound like the lady protesting too much. Let that information come naturally too. Eventually.

"You know, Trevor's at the age where he really should have other children to play with. Jordan's terribly good with him, but he has to be out doing ranch work all day. I'm afraid he'll become too attached to me, and that will be really upsetting when I leave. Do any of you with kids this age have a playgroup I could join? So he can get to know a wider world?"

"Playgroup?" A slender redhead spoke up. "What a wonderful idea. You mean like, we could get together for coffee sometimes and our kids could play together? No, we don't have anything like that, but I'd love to."

"So would I." Lois Peterson began to set out salads as she spoke. "Jamie's just that age, and he drives me crazy, just the two of us in the house all day while Len tends to his cows. The other kids are older and off to school. Even when they get home they're doing homework or riding their horses or out helping Len."

The redhead turned to Rosemary. "By the way, I'm Susan Adams. I live between you and Lois. Well, why don't we start one? Tinker Bell's an only child too, like Trevor. I think it's a great idea. What about Tuesdays and Thursdays at ten? We can leave lunch prepared for the men and just have a girl day. Stay as long as we want."

The rest of the women in the circle shook their heads. They went off to jobs, or their kids were older, or both.

"Why don't you come over to Jordan's place on Tuesday then?" Rosemary asked. "I'll make some chicken salad sandwiches for lunch and maybe come up with another cheesecake."

When there were nods of agreement, she smiled and turned to Lois. "Now, what can I do to help?"

****

"Well." Jordan steered the Jeep Cherokee down the road from the Peterson ranch, "You and your cheesecake seemed to be a hit." She'd performed like a champion. Men and women both had been eating out of her hand during the barbecue.

Rosemary jerked both thumbs into the air. "Yes. Mission accomplished. At least this stage of it."

"So they're convinced you limit yourself to the kitchen and stay out of my bedroom?"

"I didn't say that. In fact, we didn't discuss that, one way or the other."

Jordan lifted his eyebrows. "No? I thought that was the whole point of this exercise."

Rosemary chuckled. "Jordan Sterling, you might be a damned fine cowboy and a wonderful father, but you've still got a bit to learn about psychology. What would you think if a man came up to you at a party and said, 'I don't beat my dog'?"

Jordan frowned, thinking about it. "Well." He nodded thoughtfully. "I guess I'd probably assume the fellow beat his dog."

"Exactly." Rosemary checked the backseat. Trevor slept quietly. Then she turned back to face Jordan. "I rest my case."

She was quite a woman. His guardian angel. For a moment he wished this future marriage could be something more. But no. That wouldn't be fair to Rosemary. And if he asked, and she refused, her only choice would be to leave, and he wouldn't even have the safety net for Trevor.

"So." Rosemary smiled at him. "How'd you get along at the party? Glad you went?"

"Yeah, I guess so." Suddenly he knew he was glad he'd gone. "Good to see the old gang again."

"They didn't make you feel awkward?"

"Hell, no. Just like I slid back into things. Just like the last five years never existed. Except that I was packing the little guy around with me. Nobody can resist the little guy. How'd you manage to charm everybody so well?"

She shrugged. "I just offered a few things that other women want. Cheesecake. An idea for staving off cabin fever. Help with the dishes."

She had a funny little grin, a cat and canary kind of grin.

"Okay," he said. "Out with it. What are you up to?"

She clapped her hands together. "A playgroup. Susan Adams and Lois Peterson both have toddlers too, and Trevor needs other children to play with. We're meeting every Tuesday and Thursday morning for coffee, then lunch. First time's Tuesday at our—I mean, Tuesday at your house."

A Freudian slip. Maybe. He wished it could be true. Why couldn't Rosemary have been the woman he met and danced with at the party after the Calgary Stampede?

Because Rosemary wouldn't have been there. Rosemary wouldn't have thrown her body at a stranger at a party. She wouldn't even be at that kind of party. Rosemary would meet men through friends or family. Maybe even church. But because of him, his ex-wife, his child, it didn't look like Rosemary had met any men at all for the last two years.

A better man, he told himself, would feel guilty about that.

In the meantime, he'd accept all the invitations they got, even throw a barbeque himself now and then. He'd give Rosemary as much of a social life as he could.

Rosemary turned toward him and laid her left hand lightly on his arm. "It's not just me. I'm doing this for you too, you know. You need to become part of the community again, and Trevor needs to grow up with friends his own age."

Chapter Seven

Jordan heard the piano as he came in after finishing the chores. For a moment, he was transported back to his childhood.

His mother had played the piano—everything from the Beatles to Bach to western ballads. When he'd come home from school, she'd often been there, fingers flying over the keys, improvising on the tunes he loved, adding trills and chords to the written music.

The melody of "The Red River Valley" drifted from the living room, haunting him. It might have been his mother's spirit come to comfort him in the twilight. This was just the way she'd played, the old tune so dressed up with extra notes and runs that it sounded more like a concert rendition than a simple cowboy song.

Sarah Sterling had been a beautiful woman, hardworking, but full of fun and laughter. On quiet winter evenings she'd often played while he did homework and his dad worked on the books, his feet tapping out the rhythm. That was before white carpet had covered the living-room floor.

What wouldn't Jordan give to turn back the clock to before the farm truck, with its load of cattle, had swerved to avoid a dog, and instead crashed into a heavy eighteen-wheeler, killing both his parents instantly.

After that he'd been alone, other than those three wretched years with Blair. Time moved on, but except for Trevor, it had brought him nothing good.

Jordan looked into the living room. A single lamp shone on the music, surrounding Rosemary with a golden halo. It was hard to remember he distrusted women. Hard to remember he'd committed himself to a do-not-touch marriage.

He paused in the doorway and stood there a moment, drinking her in—Rosemary, the music, his mother's piano. As if she sensed another presence in the room, she stopped and turned sideways on the bench to face him.

"Don't stop," he said. "I like it. That's one of the songs my mother used to play."

"Oh." She smiled softly. "That makes sense. It's in a book of old music I found in the piano bench. I guess I chose this song because I live in the Red River Valley."

He chuckled, and crossed the room. She slid over to leave room for him to sit beside her. "Wrong Red River, I suspect. I'm not sure, but I think the song is about the one in Texas."

"I see. I always wondered about that."

In the glow of the single light, her beauty was ethereal, out of reach.

Conscious of their bodies close beside each other on the narrow bench, he knew he should get up and walk away now, while he still could. Touching her was forbidden. He would have to work patiently to build up trust and friendship, and remember that those were all.

Friendship was the most he had to offer. He'd sworn that he'd never again share his soul with another person. Sure, he was attracted to her, but that was all. Too bad he had so much trouble convincing his body of that.

His hand reached out as if it wasn't connected to his brain. Hesitantly, gently, reverently, he touched her hair. With the tips of his fingers, he stroked the ends and watched the golden strands flow across his hand. Their silken texture seemed to worm its way into his very being—into his blood, his body and his heart.

His good intentions disappeared like dew into the morning sun. "Rosemary." The word hovered in the air like a gentle breath. He swung to face her. "You're beautiful. God, you're so beautiful."

She turned toward him without answering. Her calm eyes searched his face, and her lips parted in a half-smile.

"Rosemary. I'm sorry." He lied. Yes, his brain was sorry, the brain that told him he owed her, the brain that reminded him he'd be in a tough spot if she left him, the brain that told him that he would never convince Rosemary to go through with this marriage if he hit on her like a sex-crazed maniac.

His body listened to the sensual message from his fingertips that said her hair was soft as spun gold, her scent as enticing as the flower in her name, her body as desirable as the apple in the Garden of Eden.

His fingers continued caressing as the voice of his brain said once more, "I'm sorry."

She shook her head. "It's all right." She paused. "So far."

Whatever that meant. But he thought he knew. Just a little more touching. Nothing else.

He stroked the side of her face. With his thumb, he felt the little dimple beside her eye, and traced the spot where later in life, laugh lines would appear. They would be laugh lines—he knew that. Rosemary brought joy and happiness to everything she touched.

She eased closer and moved her hands up to cradle his head, running her fingers through his hair, making the short strands at the back of his neck stand straight up. He relaxed into her. If time could freeze this moment, he would stay here in Rosemary's arms forever, her fingers tousling his hair, her hands stroking his neck.

"You're an angel. My own guardian angel."

She cuffed him lightly. "Don't be silly. I'm no angel. Just a damned good nanny." She lowered her hands, but left her body pressed against his. "Jordan, I've told you time and time again, you need to work less and relax more." She caught his hand and spread it out in both of hers. "Just look at you—tense as a newly-tuned piano string." She traced the outlines of his fingers, then kneaded them one by one.

"Feels wonderful." He exhaled with pleasure.

"Yes." She released his hand and tapped him between the shoulders. "Now, just turn your back to me."

When he obeyed, she hooked her hands over his shoulders from the back and probed and circled with her thumbs until his knotted muscles began to soften and relax. Then she moved her palms downward and made wide circles, pausing on each clump of tight muscles to make a fist and pummel the knots with her knuckles.

Rosemary was a giver, not a taker. Bit by bit she had given back to him everything he had lost—his son, a home that was a good place to come back to, even nutritious meals and a relaxed atmosphere.

Her hands roamed over his back and shoulders,

bringing comfort and healing. First, they brought comfort and healing. Then they brought unbearable desire. She smelled good, and she tasted good. He couldn't help wanting her.

Stop this, cowboy, his conscience told him. *Stop it before you get in over your head. Before you spook her for good.*

He didn't listen. He touched her breast tentatively, hoping she'd consider it an accident. He heard her sharp intake of breath, felt the quickening of her heartbeat.

He heard her gasp. "No!" She lowered her hands and scuttled across to the far side of the piano bench.

"Out of bounds?"

"Afraid so."

"You're not angry?"

"Not really. I've no reason to be angry. But it's time to quit."

"You won't leave?"

She took a deep breath, shook her head. "No. I said I'd stay and I will."

What could he say? *Thank you* seemed inadequate. "You're a good woman, Rosemary," he managed finally.

"The meal's in the oven. I'll eat later." She stood, then escaped through the door.

****

Rosemary fled from Jordan and the piano. She scurried toward her room, then remembered Trevor was asleep, so she swerved into the study and flung herself onto the sofa. Damn him anyway. And damn her own traitorous body! What would have happened if she hadn't come to her senses and pushed him away?

Would they have had wild wonderful sex now? And if that happened would they become platonic the moment they married? Hah!

Thank goodness she'd recovered her judgment in time.

She couldn't leave. She'd promised to enter into this absurd contract, and she prided herself on keeping her word. Besides, it was all for Trevor anyway. That hadn't changed.

She'd made a good start on becoming part of the community, she reminded herself. That was far more important that a bit of temporary passion.

****

Tuesday morning, Rosemary hummed lightly as she cleaned the kitchen, and made sandwiches. The cheesecake sat ready in the fridge.

When the sandwiches were ready and covered with a damp dishcloth and some plastic wrap to keep them fresh, Rosemary brought out a large comforter from the linen closet and spread it on the living room floor to protect the carpet. Then she added two sheets to protect the comforter.

She chuckled to herself. Bet Blair never dreamed when she installed the white carpet that babies would play on it.

The doorbell rang and Rosemary opened the door. Lois and Susan, with their toddlers, stood on the front steps.

"Come in." Rosemary took their coats and led them into the living room. "I thought we'd just put the kids on the floor to play while we drink coffee and chat."

"There you go, Tinker Bell." Susan plunked a red-haired toddler down in the middle of the sheets and dumped a container of plastic toys beside her. Jamie Peterson joined them.

"Is her name really Tinker Bell?" Rosemary asked.

Susan's grin was infectious. "We named her after me, actually. But don't you think she looks like Tinker Bell? When she goes to school she'll probably become Susie."

Rosemary laughed and brought Trevor and all his plastic farm animals to join the group, then poured coffee.

She heard all about the trials and tribulations of being a ranch wife, and asked advice about potty training. It was time, she knew, because she didn't want Jordan to be stuck with a baby in diapers when she left, but she didn't know anything about it. Lois had plenty of advice and Susan listened as raptly as Rosemary, since Tinker Bell wasn't potty trained yet either.

In turn, Rosemary explained what she did as a marketing consultant.

Susan pursed her lips. "But how can you do that out here?"

"All I need is my computer and a phone connection."

Rosemary glanced at the three toddlers. Each was absorbed in building blocks, nesting toys, and plastic animals. "Come on and I'll show you. It's all just down the hall."

Lois looked around the room as they walked. "The house has changed a lot since I was last in here. That was before Jordan was married."

"Oh, yes. Blair was quite the decorator." Rosemary shook her head and laughed. "Do you want a tour of the whole house?"

They did, and Rosemary wanted to give them one. Coffee cups in hand, they followed her through the dining room, kitchen, laundry room, family room, with plenty of o*ohs* and *ahs*.

They passed the closed door of the master bedroom. "We'll skip Jordan's bedroom. I've free run of the rest of the house."

She turned into the room down the hall. "Here's where Trevor and I sleep. He's on the bottom bunk. I'm on the top." Both beds were made up with sheets and comforters. Some of Rosemary's clothing was slung carelessly onto chairs.

"You don't mind sharing a room with a baby?" Susan cast her a skeptical look.

Rosemary shrugged. "I'm used to it and he's still pretty little. If I were staying longer, I'd probably move into the spare room, but for now, this is handy. I can hear him if he cries. The bathroom's right next door, and we have it to ourselves since the master bedroom has its own bath."

No, ladies. I don't mind you finding out I share my room with a baby. Regardless of what your suspicions were.

****

A few days later, Jordan took them riding again, with Rosemary on Molly and Trevor held snugly in front of Jordan on Satan. This time Rosemary had looked forward to the excursion, sure that Molly had no intention of breaking into frantic gallops or skittering wild-eyed after every passing partridge.

Rosemary had been at the Sterling ranch for over three weeks. It was now mid-June, so hay and wildflowers carpeted the meadows. The scent of wild roses still hung on the air. The sun shone out of a blue sky, and the leaves had shed their pale apple green for the lush emerald of summer. If only they could last forever, these idyllic days. If only she could share this ranch with Trevor and his father, forever.

Rosemary pointed to a herd of horses in the distance. "Nice horses." There must have been forty or fifty of them. "They're yours?"

"Yes," Jordan said. "My pride and joy. Purebred quarter horses. My hobby used to be training and showing them, but afraid I've been so busy lately that they're just grass-burners."

Rosemary sat quiet on old Molly, admiring the horses, admiring the mountains, admiring Jordan Sterling.

He was a damned desirable hunk of man right now. What had he been like before he lost his parents? Even when Blair met him? The young cowboy who trained and showed quarter horses, who rode a prize stallion in the Stampede parade, who danced and laughed and flirted. Before life with Blair had turned him into a recluse and a workaholic.

Wouldn't Rosemary love to peel away the layers of bitterness and find the real Jordan Sterling? His son had begun to give him back his life. But wouldn't she love to see him reclaim the rest of it, to become again the young man he still was in chronological years, to train and show his horses, to laugh and flirt and love.

****

Jordan waved a piece of toast in front of Trevor to distract him from blowing bubbles in his milk. The news from Manitoba wasn't as good as last week's had been. Roscoe and Blair were getting ready to leave the motel, apparently having given up finding Trevor near Rosemary's parents.

Yesterday's jaunt on horseback had gone very well. Rosemary said she enjoyed it. Jordan glanced across the table at Rosemary. She looked happy this morning. Sort of like a farm cat that had just discovered an unending supply of gourmet mice. "Just won the lottery?"

"Not really. Why don't you put Trevor in his playpen

after he's fed and changed? I've something to run by you."

Hmm. Had she decided she wanted to share his bed? Not likely. When he'd settled Trevor in the playpen with his favorite toys, Jordan refilled coffee cups and rejoined Rosemary. "Okay. What is it?" Hopefully she wasn't thinking of leaving. He didn't think that would make her so happy.

"I've been thinking…"

"Dangerous. Dangerous. Dangerous."

"Shut up, Jordan Sterling." She grinned at his teasing, though. "No. I've mentioned this before, but I think it's time. I think you should hire some help. Now." She smiled at him with all her teeth. "Remember, Sidney Perkins advised the same thing."

"You know, I've decided to do that. I think it's also time for the formal engagement. Especially if there's a risk of Roscoe and Blair closing in on us. You've been here a month now. Surely that's long enough for you to have fallen in love with such a handsome fellow as myself."

She allowed him a small chuckle. "So what's your point?"

"My point is that we can kill two birds with one stone. Get engaged. Hire a man—maybe not a top cowboy—not yet anyway. Just a laborer who's willing to work as a ranch hand, if I can find one who hasn't rushed off to Fort McMurray to slog in the oil patch. You've seen those two vacant bungalows down the driveway? They used to have families in them when my folks were alive— the ranch foreman and one year-round cowboy. Other than that we hired extras in busy times."

They sat a moment in silence.

"Tell you what," Jordan said. "Why don't we drive into Calgary Thursday afternoon? Tomorrow I'll call the employment office and tell them I'm looking for someone and let them know what time I'll be around, so they can get a few people for me to interview. You can help if you like, unless Trevor starts fussing. Then we can go ring shopping and have dinner? How's that sound?"

"Sounds wonderful." Her mind raced. She loved Trevor to death, but it had been an eternity since she'd had a real honest-to-goodness date. Just herself and a good-looking man. "I've got an even better idea. I'll phone

Susan and Lois and see if I can leave Trevor with one of them. We sort of agreed at our morning coffee klatches to do this for each other. Then we can have a real day out."

"You need a vacation from Trevor?"

Rosemary wasn't sure whether he'd intended the remark to be critical. She sighed. "Jordan, you might not realize this, but I haven't had a single day away from Trevor since Blair brought him home from the hospital. She had time off—lots of it, but I didn't. Don't get me wrong. I love Trevor. I love being with him. But all mothers—even real ones—need some vacation time."

"Sorry." He nodded in apparent understanding. "I know you've given up a lot for him. No real mother could have done more. Will he sleep in a strange place?"

"Sure," Rosemary answered. "We'll take his folding playpen. If he fusses a bit, the sky won't fall. Both Susan and Lois are very capable. I'll try Susan first. Thursday's coffee meeting is at her place, so there shouldn't be a problem. He can just stay on when Lois goes home."

"Go ahead and call. And while you're at it, see if one of them would keep him late. Then we can go to a nice restaurant for dinner and find somewhere to dance later. After all, we don't get engaged every day."

Dancing? What heaven. She hadn't been out dancing for two years. "I'd love to. I'll call right away. I know it's early, but they're always up at the crack of dawn, the same as we are."

She was back in a few minutes. "No problem. Susan's very keen. Says I owe her one now and she can't wait to corner Chuck and make him take her out to wine and dine and dance."

Instead of racing to her computer, Rosemary tiptoed into her room. Trevor was still asleep. Moving quietly, she examined her wardrobe. Something simple enough to interview applicants. Something nice enough for an evening out. She had a silk suit in pale purple with a short straight skirt and a matching print blouse. She'd brought it from Winnipeg, where she'd worn it on those rare occasions when she interviewed clients face to face. It was a classic style that wouldn't scream *out of date, out of date* even though it was. A pair of fancy earrings and high-heeled shoes, and it would do just fine.

She was going out. Actually going out. Dinner and dancing. With a man. Not a date exactly. Not quite. But probably as close as she'd get for a long while yet.

Humming softly, she held the suit, still on its hanger, up against her, then, stepping into the hall with it so as not to disturb Trevor, she closed her eyes, clutched the suit, and did a few slow dance steps.

****

Jordan knocked lightly on the study door, watching as Rosemary turned and glanced up at him. "Hi. May I come in?"

"Oh. Oh. It's you."

"No. Actually it's Richard Gere." He cleared his throat. "Apologies for being late with the last bulletin from Sidney Perkins."

"So. What's new?"

"Not much, except that they've left the motel and have apparently headed back to the city. The PI will continue to follow them—which is apparently about as difficult as following an asphalt road in the wilderness. And now why don't we forget about all that and think about us."

He brought his hand from behind his back and handed her a glass jar filled with an arrangement of wildflowers—white daisies, deep pink wild roses, golden tiger lilies. "For the bride to be. Best I could do on short notice."

"Oh. Thank you." She took them from him, burying her nose in them, as if she were reveling in the scent of the roses. Then she set them aside. "Now, if you'll excuse me, I think I'd better get to work." She turned her back and placed her hand on the mouse.

Jordan lingered, eyes glued to the hair tumbling around her shoulders, to the vulnerable patch of neck that showed in a spot where the hair had parted. He should leave now. He'd been dismissed. She wanted him gone. So what was his problem? Nothing, except the little devil sitting on his shoulder with a bow and arrow, the bow strung, the arrow pointing at his heart. "You're tired?"

She nodded and returned to her typing.

"Hmm," he said. "I think I owe you one backrub, don't I?"

She didn't answer, but she began the process of shutting off the computer.

His mind told him to leave now. Fast. To quit while he was ahead. Or maybe before he got further behind. That other backrub, the one he owed her for, had led to him eating dinner by himself. His heart wasn't in a listening mood.

Once the computer sat silent, its black plastic case firmly closed, Rosemary slumped forward, elbows on the desk, chin resting on the backs of her laced fingers.

Jordan reached out and clutched the points of Rosemary's shoulders in his hands, making circles with the balls of his thumbs.

She didn't spring up and slap him. In fact, the sound that came from her throat sounded very much like a purr. When he kneaded the fronts of her shoulders at the same time as he rotated his thumbs, the purring intensified.

"Here," she said. "Up here," and pointed to the knob at the top of her spine.

He moved his thumbs to massage the back of her neck. The purrs turned to groans of pleasure. Once he'd thoroughly rubbed that area, he stooped over and moved his hands lower.

"This is awkward." He grunted. "Why don't you move over to the sofa and lie on your stomach?"

When she murmured her agreement and was settled, he sat beside her, his thigh pressing against hers on the narrow couch. He tried to blank his mind, to concentrate on the rhythm of his hand and knuckles seeking out and manipulating the tired and knotted muscles. Rosemary's eyes were shut, her breath going in and out softly as if she were asleep. Jordan stopped rubbing and drew back. She came drowsily awake and rolled over, looking up at him with muzzy eyes. His eyes fastened on her lips, full and sensual.

Could any man help himself when a woman looked at him that way? He slipped off the sofa, onto his knees beside her, cupped her dear face in his hands and covered it with light kisses, kisses that hovered, touched, roamed, hovered and touched again.

Rosemary tangled her hands in his hair and drew his head toward her.

"Rosemary," he murmured. "Rosemary. Darling." His kisses stopped hovering and touching, and fastened on her mouth.

Sweeter than honey. A trite and over-used figure of speech. But true, oh, so true.

He placed his forearms on either side of her to take his weight, then set himself to the serious business of exploring the warm moist recesses and all the nooks and crannies of Rosemary's mouth. She lay between his arms, passive, unmoving. Her hands stayed tangled in his hair.

She made no active response to the roving of his lips and tongue, but her contented passivity showed acceptance. Occasionally a soft moan escaped her, which told him that she welcomed his attentions.

He left her mouth and gazed on her half-closed eyes, and on the fanning out of her mink-brown lashes. Her lips remained parted, lush and inviting.

"Oh, Rosemary, sweetheart." The words were torn from him.

He eased himself back, so that with his tongue he could roam the hollows behind her ears, the lovely curve of her throat, the depression at the base of it.

He savored the racing of her heart. She was awake, aware of his every move, enjoying it.

He'd not yet gone past the prologue. He remembered what a single touch on her breast had brought last time. He couldn't raise the curtain on Act One, but that didn't mean there couldn't be a longer introduction.

Moving one arm carefully away from her body, he began to undo the top buttons of her shirt, exposing creamy skin and the beginnings of the swell of breasts.

He kissed and nibbled from the base of her neck, down across the ridges of the breastbone. His elbow lay lightly on her stomach, and through it he could feel the beginnings of rhythmic contractions in her stomach muscles. He thought about exploring those soft and creamy breasts.

No. Absolutely not.

He stood up, which restored bits of his sanity.

"I think I'd better leave you to go to sleep." His voice sounded thick, hoarse.

Rosemary sat up straight. "Yes." She looked at him

wide-eyed. "We've got to stop this. I know I led you on again, but that was wrong."

"Uh, why?" Dumb question. He knew why.

"We're busy figuring out how to show that Blair is an unfit mother, right? This isn't the way to do it. Maybe no one would ever know, but that doesn't matter. We know it's wrong."

She was right. They were looking for evidence that Blair was having affairs rather than looking after her child as a good mother should. He stumbled out the door. He didn't need a ranch hand. He needed a live-in housekeeper. One that spent all her waking hours watching the two of them, then slept on an air mattress between their two rooms.

Well, he wasn't likely to find one of those, and so far Rosemary hadn't been too successful at acting as her own chaperone. Not until things had already gotten out of hand.

It was up to him. He'd done very well lately, ever since the night at the piano. It was resolution time. Again. No more bringing flowers. No more wandering into her study late at night. No more intimate conversations unless Trevor was in the vicinity. Maybe he should have just proposed that their marriage of convenience be traded in on the real thing. But maybe not. Her refusal would end everything.

Chapter Eight

"Know anything about ranch work, Mr. Forbes?" Jordan asked the young man sitting in front of him in the employment office on Thursday afternoon.

"I'm not a rodeo cowboy or anything, but I grew up on a farm. Not a very prosperous one, but I can drive a tractor and ride a horse. Fix fences. That sort of thing. And I'm a hard worker." He paused, gave a nervous smile. "And you can call me Ken, sir."

"You're unemployed right now?"

"Yes, sir. I worked for a lumber company—just manual labor. That's the problem. Debbie—that's my wife—and me, we quit high school to get married. We thought that's what we wanted at the time. But then the company downsized—more work done by machines. My unemployment insurance runs out soon. Debbie waits tables when I'm home to look after the baby, but once the benefits are gone, she won't make enough to support us."

"Look." He sighed. "I know this isn't what I should say at a job interview. But it's the truth. I really need this job. Any job. You hire me, I'll work hard for you. What I can't do, I'll learn."

Jordan and Rosemary didn't speak for a moment.

Ken shrugged. "I know what you're thinking. There are all sorts of jobs in the oil patch. But I don't have the skills for the good jobs. The others—I'd have to work away from home, shut up in bunkhouses with a lot of other men, probably many of them doing nothing on their off hours but drink and play cards for money. I don't want that. I love Debbie and I love my baby. I want to be with them."

Jordan leaned back and looked the kid over. Not a kid, really, but that's what he looked like. He was probably in his early twenties, but he looked eighteen. And Jordan sure understood what he was saying. What man would want to leave his child behind for days or weeks at a time? He couldn't do that if the child in question were Trevor.

He glanced at Rosemary. She gave an almost imperceptible nod.

"I'm going to take you on." He named a starting salary. "There's a house that goes with it. It's a two-bedroom bungalow. Hasn't been lived in for a few years, but it's furnished and ready to move into. Might need dusting."

Ken's Adam's apple jerked. "You mean Debbie can have her own house? All to herself?"

"Well, she'd have to share it with you." Jordan nodded and smiled. "Yeah, that's what it means. If she wants to make a few extra dollars, Rosemary can use her up at my house some or get her for occasional baby-sitting. But that's up to her. No pressure, one way or the other."

He stood and held out his hand. Ken shook hands with him. "When can you start?"

"Tomorrow, if you'd like. Debbie's job is a fill-in, on-call sort of thing, so she won't be letting anybody down."

"Fine. Give me your address. I'll be there at ten tomorrow morning with the pick-up and a horse trailer. If you can find a couple buddies to help load boxes it'll help."

****

"Satisfied?" Jordan said to Rosemary when they left.

"Very. I think those kids needed a break. Did you see how his eyes lit up at the thought of having a real house to live in?"

Jordan nodded.

"Sort of sad, isn't it?" Rosemary said. She turned to Jordan. "Now, let's forget all that. You're going to show me Calgary. Remember?"

She stopped on the sidewalk and straightened his tie, then gave it a little pat. "And did I tell you lately how handsome you are? Dark suit, white shirt. The whole bit. Just as handsome a businessman as you are a cowboy."

He laughed. "Had to try to live up to you, didn't I?"

He took her hand, hoping for the best. She left it in his. Along with the tingling, he could feel a little quickened pulse where her thumb touched his hand.

If only? If only he had met her sooner, when he'd

been young and carefree. But back in those days, he didn't have Trevor either. Whatever else, he wouldn't trade Trevor for anything in the world. This was the woman who'd given him Trevor, more surely than Blair ever had. Without Rosemary, Trevor would be with strangers, and Jordan wouldn't be aware the child existed.

No doubt that she was enjoying the evening out in Calgary. She'd said herself that she hadn't had a normal social life for two years. Of course that didn't mean she shared his tender feelings. For now, they'd better get a real ring for the pretend wedding.

****

She didn't really need a big diamond, Rosemary told him. Just a modest engagement ring and a plain gold band would do.

"How about all this play-acting you intend to do for my lawyer and your friends? If I don't buy you a nice ring, they will. Do you really want to be engaged to Lois?"

Rosemary wrinkled her nose at him and laughed. "All right." As they walked down a sidewalk in Calgary, Rosemary began to swerve toward a department store, but Jordan grasped her firmly by the elbow and steered her into an expensive jewelry shop. They stood over the display of rings in a glass case.

"So. What kind do you want?"

"Just a small solitaire, I guess." She pointed to a ring with one tiny diamond in the center. She realized, too late, that her eyes had flickered to the ring beside it—same style, but much larger. However, Jordan had no way of knowing which was the ring of her dreams.

Error. He pointed to the large one and said, "That one," to the clerk.

Rosemary protested.

"You don't like it?"

"Well, yes," she admitted. "I love it, but—"

"But it's too expensive. Right?" He spoke into her ear so the clerk couldn't hear. "Listen," he said. "Nothing's too good for Trevor's new mom. And don't worry about the cost. The oil company can afford it."

He placed it on her finger for size, which was as perfect as the style. She gazed at it, then held it up and caressed her cheek with it. "It's beautiful, Jordan. Thank

101

you."

"You're welcome." He grinned. "And now for the wedding bands."

"You want one too?" She hadn't been sure he would want visible chains tying him to a wife who was really just the nanny and a temporary one at that.

"Of course I want one too. What did you think?"

"It's not a given, like for women," she reminded him. "I think men still have the option."

"Okay. So my option is for a wedding ring. Unless you're not okay with that?"

"Of course, I'm okay with it. Whatever you want."

They chose two wide gold bands and left the store, the wedding rings in their box, the diamond on Rosemary's finger.

****

An hour or so later, Rosemary gazed out the window of the revolving restaurant. The city of Calgary lay below her, turning in a lazy circle beneath the evening sun. Jordan sat across from her, watching her with his piercing blue eyes. If a genie should pop out of the wine bottle that sat on their table and give her three wishes, she wouldn't have to think about it for very long. A real engagement, a real wedding, and Jordan and Trevor forever.

She'd always seen Jordan in his working cowboy clothes—not his dress ones. He was a handsome man even in those. Now he was not only dressed up, but also seemed to have dropped years. His blue eyes twinkled. A strand of rumpled dark hair fell over his forehead. It invited her to reach across the table and smooth it back into place. She squeezed her hands together in her lap to keep them out of trouble.

Just the sight of Jordan struck Rosemary like a clenched fist, squeezing all her emotions into a ball, which lay compacted and yearning at the bottom of her stomach.

It wasn't hard to see why Blair had been attracted to him—it was harder to see why she gave him up. But Blair had always been a shallow creature, easily bored. If Jordan Sterling belonged to her, Rosemary thought, she'd never let him go. His looks were the least of it. He was kind, responsible, a good father—

102

But he wasn't interested. He'd made that clear enough. Oh, yes, he'd like to get her into bed, but he'd promised not to do that. It wasn't in the contract. She lost herself in her daydreams, stroking her beautiful diamond with the thumb of her right hand.

"Rosemary—" Jordan waved his hand in front of her face. Fortunately the dim lighting prevented him from seeing how red that face was. "Earth to Rosemary."

"Sorry?"

"The waitress is ready for our order."

"Oh." Rosemary looked up at the waitress. "Sorry. It's just that your city is so beautiful—"

"Do you need more time?"

Rosemary glanced at Jordan. He shook his head.

"In Calgary, you have beef." He plucked the menu out of her hand and gave it to the waitress. "I'm having prime rib. I recommend it. Okay?"

She nodded and the waitress moved off.

"This city's built on oil," Jordan told her. "And so is this tower." He leaned toward Rosemary, pointing out each landmark in the city as the restaurant revolved.

She wanted to reach out and touch his face. The premature lines, which on the ranch she'd assumed were from worry, here became laugh lines. If the young Ken Forbes worked out, maybe, just maybe, Jordan Sterling would look like this more often.

Resolutely, Rosemary turned her mind away from her future, or lack of it. The night was warm, the moon was bright, she was wearing a pretty outfit, and it had been a long, long time since a man had taken her dining and dancing. It was almost as if they were a real couple, out on the town, celebrating their engagement.

****

"You know all the night spots in Calgary?" Rosemary asked Jordan when they were seated at a small table next to the dance floor.

"I should," he said. "I did at one time, I guess. Back before Mom and Dad were killed, I used to come to the Stampede every year, plus I came into town now and then for an evening like this with friends." He smiled, laugh lines crinkling, teeth white in the dim light. "The ladies all thought I was hot back then."

"You still are." Rosemary's impulses got the better of her. She leaned across the small table and brushed the wayward lock from his forehead, letting her fingers linger in his hair. Not that his hair didn't look right, but she had to touch him. She just had to. Light bounced off the facets of her diamond ring and made patterns on the ceiling.

"We're driving home tonight." Jordan chuckled and looked at his drink. "Do you think they'll throw me out of here if I make this one drink last forever?"

She laid her hand on his. "Not if you tip generously for your soft drinks. Or, just maybe, I could drink enough for both of us."

"Right. I can sure picture that." Did he caress her with his eyes? Or just roll them with humor? He held out his hand. "Come on. Sounds like a slow one. Let's dance."

She held her head to one side and smirked. "You can't handle fast dancing?"

"Sure." He pulled her to him. "But right now, I think slow dancing sounds like a lot more fun."

Didn't it though? Rosemary rested her head against his shoulder. When he snuggled her tight and laid his cheek against hers, she responded by lifting her hand from his lapel and looping it around the back of his neck. His neck felt prickly as if the hair had been clipped recently. Near the hairline, she could feel the outline of a small mole or scar. Absently, she circled it with a forefinger. Jordan nuzzled his lips against her ear in response.

She hadn't dated for almost two years. Was that why everything in her tingled and glowed at the touch of this man's hand? No. She'd never tingled and glowed like this even in the days when she'd had a date every Saturday night. Her breathing slowed. It was as if by stopping her breath, by stopping her heartbeat she could by sheer force of will make this moment last forever. She could freeze time, spend eternity wrapped in Jordan Sterling's arms, his breath hot on her ear, his lips questing in the hollow behind it.

They left the club relatively early because they still had to pick up Trevor and go home, The evening air was chilly, and Jordan wrapped an arm around Rosemary's shoulders as if to warm her. She pressed against his side, taking comfort from his body heat.

He opened the passenger door of the Jeep and helped her in, then went around and settled into the driver's seat. When they were out of the city, he put his arm around her again, and she snuggled her head against his shoulder.

They had the roads to themselves after they left the city. A full moon illuminated the shrubs and trees and telephone poles along the road to produce a black and white surreal landscape. Stars glittered in a cloudless sky. Rosemary sat silent, unwilling to speak and disturb the bond between them.

"It's after midnight," Jordan said. "You think Susan will be upset with us picking Trevor up?"

Rosemary looked up drowsily. "Huh uh. I told her we'd probably be making a late night of it."

"And she said?"

"She said *good*. Because that meant she could keep Chuck out all night when it was her turn. If you don't want to stop for him now, I can call her on my cell phone, then get him in the morning."

Jordan withdrew his arm and put both hands on the steering wheel. "I don't think that's a very good idea."

****

When they returned to the house after picking up Trevor, Jordan carried the child into the house, then handed him to Rosemary. Trevor or no Trevor, he wasn't about to torture himself by following Rosemary into her bedroom.

When they'd been dining and dancing, he'd let his guard down and pretended he was twenty-four again, unmarried, without responsibilities. He'd been stupid to forget he now faced a different situation. Rosemary wasn't a date to kiss goodnight and leave at her apartment door. In all ways except one, she acted like a wife. She cleaned his house, cooked his meals, cared for his child, duties she'd continue after their marriage of convenience, which would probably be a lot more convenient for him than it would for Rosemary.

He unknotted his tie and unbuttoned his white shirt, then threw both of them into the corner. He hung his suit in the closet. Maybe this time next year he'd wear it again. He'd have to buy a new one for the wedding.

He crawled between the clean sheets that Rosemary left every week at his bedroom door and lay on his back, hands propped under his head, eyes open. What if? What if he'd said that, yes, they'd collect Trevor in the morning? What if, Trevor-less, Jordan had kissed Rosemary in the entryway, in the family room, in the hall of the bedroom wing?

Would she have come with him into this room? Would she even now be beside him in the big bed, skin flushed with desire as he ran his hands down the knobs of her spine, inscribed hot circles around her stomach with his palms, caressed and kissed her breasts?

He turned over, wrapped his arms around the extra pillow and burrowed his head into his own pillow, seeking the sleep that wouldn't come and dreaming that the pillows were Rosemary's soft breasts.

What if he'd turned to her and said, *Please, Rosemary, marry me for real, till death do us part*?

And what if she had said, *Sorry, not part of the contract? And, now that the contract's been broken, I feel I have to leave.*

Rosemary wasn't for him. She deserved more than a recluse rancher with a broken marriage in his past, old before his time with work and worry. Much as she loved Trevor, she deserved a real courtship and marriage. If he asked her for a real marriage, for Trevor's sake, and if, for Trevor's sake, she agreed, how long would she be happy with her bargain?

****

Rosemary removed Trevor's hooded jacket and laid him on the lower bunk. He'd already been in his sleepers, curled up on the floor of the playpen when they'd picked him up.

In a few minutes Rosemary was stretched out in the top bunk, lights out. Silence descended on the house.

Rosemary lay on her back and pondered. Jordan had seemed to enjoy the evening, seemed to enjoy her. When they danced, he held her close. He touched her when she got out of the car, when she got into the car, when she sat down at the table or stood up to dance. Yet at the very thought of being alone in the house with her, he'd jumped like a scalded cat.

He desired her. No doubt about that. But on a strictly physical level. What was his problem? Once bitten, twice shy? Did she remind him too much of Blair?

What would happen if now, tonight, she suggested a lifetime marriage?

She snorted aloud. She'd put up with enough humiliation as it was. Having that overture turned down would be the final straw.

****

"Guess what?" Rosemary asked the next Tuesday morning to Lois and Susan while the three toddlers played on the floor. She held her left hand behind her back.

"What?" Lois and Susan spoke in unison.

Rosemary stuck out her hand, ring finger prominent. "Jordan and I are getting married."

"You're what?" Susan shrieked.

"Getting married." She flashed the ring closer to their faces and gave them a smug smile as they oohed and aahed.

They slid their chairs closer to Rosemary's to form a coffee klatch version of a football huddle.

"Tell all," Lois said.

Rosemary shrugged. "Nothing much to tell. We just decided to get married"

Susan snorted. "Sounds about as romantic as two earthworms. Why are you marrying Jordan?"

"Well…" Rosemary ducked the question. "Why did you marry Chuck?"

Susan roared with laughter. "That's easy. I had my eye on his body ever since high school, but he wouldn't give it to me until he had a ring on my finger. Not the equivalent of your rock either. The wedding band. Can you imagine? The *man* holding out for marriage?"

A shadow passed over Rosemary's heart. Jordan had held out for marriage with Blair. He'd loved Blair. He didn't even pretend to love Rosemary. She wiggled like a horse flicking off flies, then laughed. "Well, about the same reason, I guess."

"What? When you've been living together forever—well, almost two months anyway—you can't get the man

107

into bed until you marry him?"

"Jordan's very conservative, really." Rosemary defended him instinctively.

"So when's the wedding?" From Lois.

"What are you wearing?" From Susan.

Rosemary shrugged and spread her hands. "Soon. What am I wearing? I don't know. Something simple. We're just getting married. It's not a big deal."

Susan made a noise somewhere between a groan, a shriek, and a snort. "Not a big deal!"

"Well, after all, it's not a first wedding for Jordan."

"But it is for you, isn't it? A first wedding? You haven't been married before have you?" Susan asked.

Rosemary shook her head, a half-smile on her lips.

Susan took over the conversation while Lois seemed content for the moment to sit back and listen. "Well, it's the bride who calls the tune. She's the one having the big day. Besides, I don't think you can count Jordan's first time. I don't think he even had a wedding. She dragged him to the nearest justice of the peace, I imagine, before he could get away. All I know is one day she came here and everything changed. Nobody ever saw her, and we hardly ever saw him again. The woman was a barracuda. You can't count it as a wedding when a barracuda swallows you, can you?"

"Susan!" Lois interrupted the tirade. "You don't seem to know the difference between a barracuda and a whale. And remember, she's Rosemary's sister."

"I don't care," Susan said. "It's the truth. Rosemary probably knows it even more than we do. I never met the woman and I hated her. If I'd gotten to know her, I'd probably have liked her even less." She took a deep breath. "No, Lois. Rosemary's our friend and she's having a wedding she'll remember."

Rosemary sat back, stunned, with what she hoped was an enthusiastic smile frozen on her face.

"Okay—" Susan dug a note pad and pen from her purse. "Date? We need at least a month. Well, three weeks anyway. Date, Rosemary?"

"Uh," Rosemary said. "I guess I'd better check with Jordan."

"Forget Jordan." Susan shook her head. "It's your

show. What about the next to last Friday in August?" She jotted down the date.

Yes, Rosemary knew she should be offended at the way these two friends took over, but she wasn't. Somewhere in the back of her mind, she'd always treasured the idea of the walk down the aisle, the bridesmaids, the long white dress. She would never have suggested all this herself, but it was easy to sit back and let the tide of plans wash over her.

The wedding night might never arrive, but the wedding day could be one to remember. It would also help validate this marriage in the eyes of a judge and of the community—the community that Trevor would be part of for the rest of his life.

The two women went on and on. Jordan's ranch house would be better than a church as Rosemary was new here and hadn't chosen a church yet. Lois's second cousin was an assistant pastor in Calgary. He'd come if she asked him. Rosemary had to let her parents know at once, so there'd still be time to change the date if they couldn't come. Or if the second cousin couldn't come. Or if Jordan had a conflict.

No, Rosemary didn't have anyone from Winnipeg she wanted for her bridesmaid. The friends decided Susan would be the bridesmaid. She was closer to Rosemary's age. Lois would be in charge of the reception. Rosemary needn't worry about a thing except supplying the names of any friends or relatives she wanted to invite to add to the list of neighboring ranchers Susan busily scribbled down.

Invitations? Susan agreed time was short. Maybe Rosemary could make one up on the computer. Could she do it right away so that when the three of them went to Calgary next week to shop, they could make photocopies?

"But—" Rosemary tried to interject at one point.

"It's OK," Lois said. "You don't need to worry about anything except the invitation. Your parents can stay with mine. I think you said your dad was a doctor—so's mine. Retired. They'll have a lot in common."

Rosemary spread her hands before her, palms up. She was relieved. If her mother stayed with her, it would be hard to convince her that nothing was wrong. However, she felt like she had to put up a token protest. "But they can stay here. There's a guest bedroom."

"No," Lois said firmly. "If they stay with you, your mother will insist on scrubbing all the floors and filling the freezer with apple pies. I know mothers. They need a vacation too. My folks will love showing them around." She continued, "I'll call my cousin as soon as I get home. Belinda's boyfriend will run the video camera. We'll let you pick out the wedding dress, but otherwise, it's in our very capable hands. Is money a problem?" Belinda was Lois's teenaged daughter.

Rosemary shook her head. "No. My business is successful with a low overhead. I can pay for my own wedding."

"That's good. Most of the food will be donated, but you can splurge on clothes. We'll pick out a hotel for the honeymoon and make reservations for you. One of us can keep Trevor for a few days."

"No." Rosemary remembered that they didn't know about Ken and Debbie yet. "You won't have to. I convinced Jordan to hire a man to help on the ranch. His wife is good with Trevor, so I think that's covered."

The focus of interest swung to this new development.

"Who is he?"

"What's she like?"

"Will they be permanent?"

"Do you like her?"

Rosemary took a deep breath. "Actually, I invited her to come this morning. She has a toddler too. But she had some things she wanted to do. You'll meet her Thursday. She said she'd come then."

As they left, they both kissed Rosemary. "Any changes," Lois said. "You let us know right away. Decide what day you want to go to town next week to shop for clothes, and give me a call. Okay?"

Whew! Rosemary's head spun faster than the rides at a country fair.

The wedding might even take her mind off the marriage.

Chapter Nine

"Uh—" Rosemary began when she and Jordan sat down to dinner. "There's something I have to tell you."

"What?"

"Well—let's just put it this way. Are you busy on the next-to-last weekend of August?"

"Why?"

"Lois and Susan picked that Friday for our wedding. I phoned my mom and dad. They can make it then. Although they were surprised, to put it mildly. Lois phoned her second cousin and he can make it too."

Jordan's eyebrows shot up. "Lois's second cousin?"

"He's an assistant pastor somewhere in Calgary."

"I see. And what else have Lois and Susan planned?"

Rosemary spread her hands. "Absolutely everything. They said I had a right to pull out all the stops, since I haven't been married before. And they didn't seem to think the fact you had meant anything either. I don't think a bride who hasn't been properly inspected and approved by the neighbors counts for much around here. The wedding will be here at the house and so will the reception."

"Uh huh. The house, eh?" She'd been concerned Jordan would be annoyed at the uncontrolled avalanche loosed upon them, but his lop-sided smile indicated more amusement than anything. "So your simple wedding has gotten out of hand, has it?"

"Oh, no." She didn't want him to worry. "Not at all. These are two efficient women. All we need do is show up."

"Ah." Jordan looked as though he was trying not to grin. "Are they taking care of the honeymoon too? I'm assuming you didn't share the truth about that with them."

"Of course not!" Rosemary felt herself flush. "I know I don't lie well, but if I just pretend I'm acting, I think I can

111

put up a good front. And, yes, they're taking care of the honeymoon. Weekend reservations in some hotel in Calgary. So if you want any choice, you'd better tell them now. Tomorrow may be too late. I can express an opinion about the gown, but they're taking me shopping in Calgary next week, and I'm told it's to be long and white. More going-away outfits than Barbie and enough neg—, er, other things, to equip a harem."

"Negligees?"

"I could hardly object, could I? They'd suspect something. But don't worry. You won't have to look."

"Rosemary." Jordan stalled her torrent of words. "Do you want this? You're not just letting them steam-roll you? You really want this?"

"Yes." She nodded. "I wouldn't have taken it on myself, with no family here. But yes, I want it. I've always wanted it."

She paused. "Besides, it makes the right impression." She couldn't resist adding, "Isn't that what Sidney wants?"

"All right. Then I want it too."

The man was totally deaf when it came to sarcasm. "The only thing I was worried about is do you think it's safe to wait that long? According to the lawyer, I mean?"

"Yes, I think so. He sort of gave me the impression that a formal engagement would do. And I'm sure the wedding you're describing looks much more legitimate than what I had in mind."

"To us." She raised her glass. "To us, and to the neighbors, and to the judge and the social workers and to successful deceit." She added caustically, "And to Sidney."

Jordan clinked his glass against hers. "To us. And did they ask why we were marrying?"

Rosemary swallowed. "Oh, yes. I told them it was the only way I could get you into my bed."

"The woman who cannot tell a lie," Jordan murmured.

"Not lying. Acting." She raised her glass again. "To us. To weddings. To Trevor. To a long and successful acting career by the woman 'who cannot tell a lie.'"

She turned from him sharply before he could see the look on her face. See that the actress was nearing the end of her script.

Trevor looked up, intrigued by this new game. "Da-dee. Da-dee," he chortled. "Da-dee. Aunty Wose. Aunty Wose. Da-dee."

"Oh, dear," Rosemary said to the wall. "He's just got Aunty Wose almost perfected, and soon I'll have to start on Mommy."

She added, "After all, the neighbors will expect it."

****

"Want to come for a picnic in the hills?" Jordan asked Rosemary over breakfast.

Rosemary looked up from her poached eggs and toast. Her heart thumped. "Today?"

"Yep, today. Make a day of it. I'll pack a picnic lunch, and we'll go on horseback to a spot several miles out in the far pasture where there's a mountain meadow covered with wild-flowers."

"Oh," she said. "Oh, yes. I guess I'd like that. I'd better get the kitchen cleaned and pack a lunch."

He shook his head. "Huh uh. This is your day off. All day. You haven't had a day off since you came here. I'm packing the lunch and doing what needs done in the kitchen."

"But Trevor?"

"You think I can't handle Trevor and the kitchen stuff both? You do it every day." He chuckled. "Come on, Rosemary. Don't be sexist. Give me an hour. You can do some of your own work, or sit in the sun, or polish your toenails, or whatever you like. Day off." He stood, and came behind her to lightly massage her shoulders. "All day."

A whole day off. Just to ride with Jordan and Trevor. To eat food someone else had prepared. To lie back amongst wild flowers with her hand over her eyes to shade them from the sun. To enjoy Trevor, with someone else taking care of the dressing, the feeding, the cleaning up.

Right now, she intended to fill the tub with warm water and bubble bath, and loll back in decadence for at least half of her hour. She intended to pamper herself, without one ear positioned for a whimper from the playpen or the lower bunk.

When the tub was full, she tested the water, then dropped her clothes and stepped in, lying back with a contented sigh.

So what was Jordan up to today? Would this be another time like that night in Calgary, where he forgot his worries and the never-ending work that plagued him? Would he laugh with her, tease her, put his arm around her shoulders and reach for her hand? Would his hair fall boyishly over his forehead, his worry lines change to laugh lines? Would he suddenly look five years younger, as he had that night?

She closed her eyes and let the water and the bubbles caress her body like the hand of a lover. For a moment, she let herself imagine that the hand belonged to Jordan Sterling.

Her eyes snapped open. She had to get a grip on herself. He'd probably feel physical attraction for Dracula's grandmother, considering what his lifestyle had been for the last two years.

She stepped from the tub and dried herself, then polished her nails, fingers and toes as he'd suggested. It might be a funny way of getting ready to ride horseback, but she'd had so little chance to pamper herself this way.

Quickly, she rummaged in her closet and pulled out an old pair of jeans, a flannel shirt, and a heavy white pullover. When she entered the kitchen, Jordan was stowing sandwiches in a backpack.

"I'd better find a jacket for Trevor," Rosemary said.

Jordan laughed. "Just relax. Nothing to do today. Remember. I can take care of the little guy. Honest. I'm his father. Remember. I'm going to be taking care of him for a long time."

And I'm not, once this farce of a marriage is over. Timely reminder.

Trevor stood in his playpen watching the proceedings.

"But the kitchen..." Rosemary tried again. "The dishes..."

"Relax, I told you."

"We can't go off and leave dirty dishes. It's depressing to come home to."

He chuckled. "Maybe. Who knows? Maybe the

brownies will do them while we're gone."

She snorted. "Yeah, right. When's the last time the brownies ever did anything for you?"

"Well, you never know, do you? Anyway, it's not your problem this time. If we come home to dirty dishes, I'll load the dishwasher. Got it?"

"Got it."

Satan pranced and snorted as Jordan reined him back to keep pace with Molly. The two horses moved side-by-side. Trevor sat up straight clutching the saddle-horn, held secure by Jordan's arm.

Rosemary took a deep breath of the fresh mountain air.

They rode past rippling streams with golden cowslips winking and beckoning on the shining surface of the water, and bright bluebells swinging by the banks.

"It's beautiful," Rosemary said to Jordan. "Just beautiful."

"Glad you like it." His eyes laughed at her from beneath the black Stetson. "That's how I feel. I could never leave this place. Never bear losing it. It's been passed from father to son for four generations now, and I finally have what I'd given up on—a son of my own to pass it to."

His face sobered. "I owe that to you, Rosemary, and I'll never forget it. My whole reason for living, I owe to you."

Rosemary's heart thundered beneath her flannel shirt. Was he about to say something wonderful and personal now? Was that why he'd brought her here? It was that kind of day. That kind of place. The hills soared skyward. The white and purple mountains loomed so close they looked to be only a short walk away.

The path narrowed, and Jordan rode ahead. The trail followed a mountain stream which meandered through a narrow valley that soon widened into a meadow covered with spring grass and wild flowers.

Jordan reined in Satan, waiting for Rosemary to ride up beside him.

"It's beautiful." She had to catch her breath at the riot of color around them. "I don't think I've ever seen anything quite so lovely."

"This is the place I chose for lunch."

For lunch? Just for lunch?

She sighed. "And thou?"

Jordan looked at her, bewildered. "Run that by me again."

A loaf of bread, a jug of wine and thou. Omar Khayyam's wish list for happiness. "It doesn't matter." She looked away and shook her head. "It's just a quotation from an old poem."

****

Jordan swung off his horse, then lifted Trevor down. The child sat on Jordan's shoulders, small legs dangling down on either side of his father's neck.

"Come on," Jordan told Rosemary. "Kick your feet out of the stirrups." He raised his arms, grasped her around the waist and pulled her to the ground.

Trevor clutched Jordan's hat and drummed his heels against Jordan's chest. "Da-Dee.Da-Dee."

"Just wander around and smell the flowers for a minute." Jordan began to unbuckle Molly's saddle. "I want to take care of the horses."

Rosemary strolled to the brook. Small wild violets grew below a willow tree that overhung the stream.

She stood with her back against the willow, breathing deeply of the scented air, and watched Jordan unsaddle the horses. When he'd finished, he spread a blanket on the ground and called to Rosemary. "Come on over and sit down."

Rosemary sat down where he'd indicated. Then he tumbled Trevor from his shoulders and placed him on the blanket near Rosemary. Trevor stood up and ran to her. They engaged in a game of roll the baby over and tickle him, Rosemary laughing and Trevor gurgling with delight.

From the corner of her eye, Rosemary saw Jordan spread another blanket and load it with plastic containers, a thermos, paper cups and plates, and a roll of paper towels.

"Come on, you two," he said then, "lunch is ready."

Trevor ran to Jordan. "Da-Dee. Da-Dee."

Jordan gave Trevor a quick cuddle, and Rosemary saw his face glow with love. He sat Trevor down beside

him and removed the top of a square container filled with
sandwiches. "Ham, chicken, or egg salad. Or some of
each." He picked out half an egg salad sandwich and
handed it to Trevor, who began to gulp it down.

Rosemary bit into a chicken sandwich garnished with
lettuce leaves while Jordan poured white wine from a
chilled thermos and brought out a small cardboard
container of milk for Trevor.

"Delicious," Rosemary said.

When they'd finished, Jordan piled the remnants of
the picnic on one corner of the blanket, then lay on his
back holding Trevor. He sang old cowboy songs until the
child fell asleep against his shoulder. Rosemary stretched
out on the other blanket, one forearm across her eyes,
shielding them from the brightness of the sun. From
under the barrier of her arm, she watched as Jordan laid
the sleeping baby on the blanket.

He then sat down by Rosemary.

"You asleep too?"

She shook her head. "Just enjoying." She slid the
protective arm up to her hairline.

"See that cloud?" She pointed. "Don't you think it
looks like an elephant? See. There's his trunk—that long
skinny cloud out to the side. And there are his ears—
they're flapping in the wind. He's running." *And there's a
cloud that looks just like the firm brow and strong chin of
Jordan Sterling.*

Jordan chuckled. "Quite an imagination. "You do this
all the time?"

"Oh, yes," she admitted. "Always. It's one of my
favorite games."

He plucked a piece of meadow grass and tickled her
nose. "Any other favorite games?"

Heavens. The man was flirting with her. Well, she
could play that game. A bit of flirting was safe. Trevor,
even asleep, was a good chaperone.

She arched her eyebrows at him. "Maybe."

"So. What are they?" He sprawled out beside her,
propped on one elbow.

"I don't know. Who's asking?"

"An admirer."

"An admirer? Oh, my goodness. How quaint and old-fashioned."

His hand moved to cover the spot between her breasts that rose and fell with her breathing.

"Maybe the admirer likes old-fashioned women. Ever think about that?"

She batted her eyelashes at him. Actually batted her eyelashes. Funny. Flirting was like riding a bicycle. You might get a bit rusty, but apparently you never forgot. "So?" she asked. "Does the admirer think he can really find one of those?"

"Oh, yes. I think he does. I think he has. A sweet old-fashioned woman with a sweet old-fashioned name. Rosemary." He said the word so softly it became part of his breathing. "Rosemary."

"I think the admirer is wearing blinders." She placed a hand over his. Warmth flooded her as he wove their fingers together. "Old-fashioned women wear skirts, not jeans. They have black cotton stockings and wear their hair in little buns behind their heads."

"Well, let's just see. How would you look with your hair in a little bun? Eh?" He eased her mass of hair from under her neck until it lay rippling against the blanket, then moved his fingers from between hers so that he could use both hands to coil and wind it to perch on top of her head.

"I like it better the other way." He fanned it out across the blanket. "Anyway, that's not what I meant by old-fashioned." He shifted his body again so that his chest touched her side. "Old-fashioned women care for people. They are friendly and helpful. And they love children. All children. Not just their own. They're unselfish and giving."

"Sounds really dull and stuffy." Rosemary raised her chin and blew on the lock of hair that fell over his forehead.

"Oh, not at all. Old-fashioned women are also gutsy and independent. They can take care of themselves and make their own way, not asking anybody for anything."

"Really?" She tilted her head to make eye contact. "That's not the way I heard it."

"It's true. You don't believe it?"

She shook her head, lips slightly parted, inviting.

"Well, then, you don't know much about pioneer women, do you? They could drive a four-horse team, start a fire with two sticks, herd cattle, and fight off timber wolves with their bare hands."

She laughed. "Sorry. Guess that leaves me out."

"Rosemary." His eyes seemed focused on her lips.

Careful. She must not, absolutely must not, go overboard. But, oh, the yearnings his words raised in her when he flirted, to say nothing of the sight of his chiseled face, his aristocratic nose. The touch of his hand on the valley between her breasts. Maybe both of them should spend more time flirting and kissing, even if it didn't lead anywhere. Especially if it didn't lead anywhere. Spend more time being young again. Surely just a few minutes of necking wouldn't hurt, even if she knew it could never lead anywhere. She smiled and felt her eyelids grow heavy with desire. Her breath quickened.

"Your eyes are so gray," Jordan said. "Just like the clouds before a rain."

"And yours are blue. So what's your point?" But she smiled as she said it.

She wasn't propped on an elbow as he was. She lay flat on her back. She lifted one hand and tangled it in his hair. Beautiful thick dark hair. Clean and shiny. Her fingers tingled from the contact. Her whole body throbbed, and something lurched in the pit of her stomach. She pulled his head down toward hers, and touched his cheek lightly with her lips.

"Ah. So that's the game is it? I think that's a game two can play. Very nicely. Here." He rolled onto his back and carried her with him, so that she lay on top of him. Then he touched her parted lips with his. "There." He showered her lips with short light kisses. "There. And there. And there. You like that?"

"Uh huh." She levered herself up, so that she looked into his eyes. The points of her elbows dug into his shoulders. "Uh-huh, cowboy. I like that just fine." She rubbed her nose against his. "In fact, I like that so much that maybe I'd like a little more." She lowered her lips onto his, cradling his head in her hands, embracing the slight roughness of the stubble that had grown since morning.

A real man. A two shaves a day kind of man.

Her mouth touched his. Her mind exploded with sensuality. The light touch disappeared. No more flirty little comments and feathery kisses. He captured her mouth, singeing her lips with his, then tickled them with his tongue before he entered her mouth. She gasped with pleasure and groaned with delight at the sensations that shot through her body. *Oh, Jordan. Wonderful, wonderful Jordan.* Right now, she didn't feel like Trevor's mother or Jordan's contract-wife. She felt like a beautiful, sensual, desirable woman.

Jordan ran his tongue against the sensitive ridges at the top of her mouth, before he withdrew it.

"Oh," she whimpered. "Ooh. Ooh. Wonderful."

"We can't do this." Jordan groaned and turned his face to the side. "Not with Trevor right here."

She levered herself up on her elbows again. "Can't do what? Obviously we can do this. We just did."

"You know what I mean."

The moment had passed, more surely than if he'd dumped a bucket of cold water over her. She rolled off him, onto her back beside him, desperate to regain her dignity. "Yes, I know what you mean. And no, we can't do it. I never intended to. It's not in the contract."

"Then why—"

She shrugged and lied through her teeth. "Why not? It was fun." *Remember to keep your tone light, Rosemary. Regain the initiative. Don't tell the man that every time he touches you, you feel as if you've been eating prairie locoweed.*

She ran the palm of her hand across his face. "You need to enjoy life, Jordan Sterling. To remember you're young and good-looking and desirable."

He breathed deeply and threw his arm up to shade his eyes. "I have to work a ranch. I can't be a playboy."

She tickled the tip of his nose with a piece of grass as earlier he had tickled hers. "So, how many cows died this afternoon while you flirted with me?"

He nodded with a rueful smile. "You're some woman, Rosemary Robbins. My Rose. In fact, I wish—"

He broke off when Trevor whimpered.

A wave of regret washed over Rosemary. What would

Jordan have told her, or asked her? It might have been most interesting.

It might have changed her life.

****

"Oh!" Rosemary looked around the kitchen. "It's all cleaned up. How—"

"Told you." Jordan lifted Trevor from his shoulders by boosting him over his head. "Told you that sometimes the brownies take care of these things. Assuming, of course, that one leaves out a saucer of cream. Or promises one."

Suddenly she understood. "Debbie. You got Debbie to come in and clean the house while we were gone."

"Uh huh. I want you to look things over and see how she did. I told her it was a surprise for you. If you like her work we'll get her once or twice a week or whatever. Look—" He ran one finger over the counter as if to check for dust. "I know I've exploited you dreadfully. You've put your own life on hold. You've just shown me that you value fun and laughter, and you should be able to have those things, too. We'll let Debbie do some housework. Manufacture a few times to leave Trevor with her—"

"She's willing?"

"I think so. They've been living pretty frugally, and I think they could use the extra money. When she comes over here, she can bring Dennis along, and if you're busy, you can take Trevor over there."

"Of course." She turned slightly away from him, so that he couldn't read her expression. "That sounds very sensible. If you can afford it."

"I can afford it." He reached forward and touched her cheek with the tip of a forefinger. "Seeing how Ken and Debbie lived made me see that maybe what I can't afford is to ignore the problems of other people."

"Right on, there. But for me, being here has been a labor of love." She went on hastily, just so he didn't get the wrong idea. "Now I believe you said I could spend the evening working on the computer. Taking care of my customers."

"Sure. If that's what you want to do. I'll take care of Trevor and then rustle up some supper for us. I'll call you when it's ready."

Rosemary sat in the study and stared at the computer. She had a new client she should do some work for. The friend of a friend who lived in a small town outside Winnipeg. He'd had a substantial, but not huge, lottery win, and wanted to use the money to establish a small business. Rosemary was running a feasibility study on what businesses might be viable within a handy commute of his home. Somehow, though, she couldn't get her mind on the client for thinking of the implications of having Ken and Debbie next door.

She liked Debbie. Debbie and Ken were a couple of kids trying to do their best in a hard cold world. Dennis seemed a happy baby, well cared for and loved. If they'd survived on a part-time job and some unemployment insurance, how could they not succeed with a steady job, a house, and extra work for Debbie?

With luck, Jordan would have more time to spend with Trevor, and she'd also have more available time. To do what? Find new clients for her business? Spend more time with the husband who wasn't really a husband? Quality time like they'd had earlier today?

Only a married couple shouldn't have to pull back as soon as things got interesting.

****

Jordan whistled tunelessly as he assembled the ingredients for an omelet. It wasn't his idea of an evening meal, but it would suit Rosemary. This day had been his engagement gift to Rosemary.

Yes, he could afford Ken and Debbie. Ken was a real worker, no doubt about that. He'd do a lot of the routine chores. That would give Jordan more time for breaking and training horses—his real love. Selling a few of them would bring in more than enough to pay for Ken and Debbie. And the oil royalties would more than cover any shortfall in other areas.

As for Trevor's future, Jordan now had a lawyer and a private investigator working on seeing that Blair could never again threaten Trevor. Then the marriage that hadn't happened yet would be dissolved. But once Rosemary left, there'd be no more coming home to a cheerful woman, no more easy conversation over the dinner table, no more rides through mountain meadows,

122

no more—

Well, there never had been that anyway.

Rosemary. Her very name rang wind chimes in his heart.

****

The golden afternoon of Rosemary's free day drifted through dinner, raced into dusk. Rosemary shut down the computer and closed the lid. It was time to give Jordan the album. He had given her this marvelous day in the mountains. She would give him the album of Trevor's life. When the marriage ended, Jordan would have the memories it held, and she would be left with nothing.

She traced the gold leaf writing with one finger, then rested her cheek against the soft blue suede of the cover. Before she took the book to Jordan, she'd look at the pictures one more time. Choke back tears one more time. She began to open the album, then closed it. There was no need. Every picture in it was printed on her heart.

She entered the family room, the album clutched to her breasts, the knuckles of her clenched fists pressed against the book so tightly she could feel the pain. Jordan sat sprawled in his recliner, one booted heel resting on the opposite knee.

"Here. I have a present for you." She laid the book on the end table beside his chair, then turned and rushed to the kitchen so he wouldn't see the tears welling in her eyes.

Once there, she poured two mugs of coffee, slopping the hot liquid over the side because the muscles in her hands were as tensed up as if she was still gripping the album. She mopped up the spill, and wiped the bottom of each mug with a piece of paper towel which she'd painstakingly folded into quarters. Anything to delay for a few more minutes.

By the time she returned, stiff upper lip firmly zipped into place, Jordan had flipped open the album and sat entranced. With one finger, he tracked the bottom of each picture. He was oblivious to Rosemary's return, unconscious of the steaming mug sitting at his elbow. Rosemary sipped her coffee and, over the rim of the mug, watched Jordan's face, watched him pore over each moment of his baby's life. Moments he'd missed.

"Look." When he noticed her, he smiled brilliantly. "Look at him there. Isn't he cute? And there—he's in your arms at his christening. Where's Blair?"

A hot tight bitter knot formed in Rosemary's throat. "She was out with one of Trevor's hundred *uncles*."

Finally he closed the album and looked at Rosemary. "That was a beautiful thing for you to do. Did you make it for me? Or you just had it anyway and decided to give it to me?"

No, she wanted to shout. *I didn't just have it. I made it piece by piece, gluing in each precious picture, so I could give it to the man who would take away my baby, leaving me with nothing in his place.*

She couldn't say those things to him.

Instead, she shrugged. "Both, sort of. I'd have kept it if you hadn't been a good father and if Trevor hadn't been in such terrible danger. I'd have added to it. A record of Trevor's growing up." She drummed her fingers on the side of her coffee mug, then rested her hand on the top and watched faint tendrils of steam curl between her fingers.

Jordan crossed the few feet of floor separating them, placed a hand over hers and squeezed, then leaned forward to brush her cheek with his lips. "You're a beautiful woman, Rosemary Robbins. You know that? A beautiful woman with a beautiful soul. Thank you."

A beautiful soul? So what did that get her? A halo? Haloes were as cold and brittle as rhinestone tiaras compared to homes and husbands and babies.

****

Now that Debbie had taken over many of the household duties, every afternoon Rosemary imprisoned herself with her computer. For all the good it did her. Her job and the money she earned would never replace the sterile promise of her fast approaching wedding. She stood up, and prowled into the family room, alone.

She'd even lost heart for her morning playgroups with Susan and Lois and had made excuses for not attending. How could she face them and pretend everything was normal? Besides, Trevor didn't need a playgroup any more.

Trevor was at Debbie's house playing with Dennis.

Trevor had been at Debbie's house playing with Dennis every afternoon for the past week. That had been Rosemary's own idea, as if, like a vaccination, small doses of missing Trevor would make it easier when her empty marriage blew up like a prairie dust storm, leaving barren fields behind it.

However, the gradual withdrawal wouldn't work. Not for her. It might work for Trevor. He couldn't wait until after lunch when he could leave. When Rosemary walked him over, he tugged at her hand, demanding to go faster, chanting over and over, "Den-nis. Deb-bie. Den-nis. Deb-bie."

She should be pleased. She'd taught him to say the words, the same as she'd taught him to say, *Da-dee*. The same as, before she even came here, she'd painstakingly taught him to say, *Aunty Rose. Aunty Wose* was still the best he could do. Huh. She sniffed to herself as she paced the floor. He pronounced everybody else's names without any problem.

Petty of her. Plain childish and petty. She could still remember when she couldn't say Rosemary properly herself. She flopped into one of the reclining chairs and sat staring at Trevor's empty playpen and fighting waves of jealousy. The teddy bear she'd given Trevor sat abandoned in one corner, the left ear partially chewed off.

Chapter Ten

Jordan appeared promptly at two at Sidney Perkins office.

"What's up?" he asked after he'd settled himself in the client's chair across the leather-topped desk across from Sidney.

"They've gone off the radar." Sidney tapped the eraser end of his pencil on his blotter.

"Huh? Run that by me again."

"Blair and Roscoe. The PI lost them. But he did discover that Blair consulted a lawyer to find out what would happen if she found Trevor."

"And?"

"And, as his birth mother, other things being equal, her getting him would be pretty much a sure thing. But everything isn't equal and that would be your argument. You have the ranch, a nice home, you're part of a community. You'll soon be married to a highly suitable woman."

"Any indication they're heading here?"

"None. They could be. They could be in Texas. Or Alaska. But we can't depend on either of the last two."

****

The next week was a whirl of activity.

On the dot of nine, on Monday morning, Susan and Lois screeched up to the door in Susan's SUV, and tumbled Rosemary into the vehicle. At the doorway of Debbie's cottage, they dumped off their toddlers.

Debbie, forewarned by Rosemary, stood in the door holding Dennis by one hand and Trevor by the other.

"It's okay?" Lois asked anxiously. "That's an awful lot of toddlers, and we'll likely be away all day."

Debbie smiled cheerfully. "It's just fine. Rosemary and I already talked it over. It's just so wonderful to have a house, and for Dennis to have kids to play with. And Jordan's taking his cell phone out with him today, and if I have any problem at all, I'm to phone him."

Rosemary felt warmed from the cockles of her heart, if there really were such things, and to the far reaches of her toes. She sighed. She was marrying the most wonderful man—for all the wrong reasons.

She scrambled into the front seat with Susan, and Lois sat in back, leaning forward to take part in the conversation.

"I know the perfect store," Susan said. "It's where I got my wedding dress. And you said that price doesn't matter?"

Rosemary nodded.

Susan turned her head toward the backseat and grinned. "Aren't we going to have fun, Lois? All those beautiful clothes, and money no object."

The store was fashionable and expensive.

Living vicariously, Lois and Susan insisted on Rosemary trying on a dozen different dresses. They were happily enough married they'd never do this again themselves, but they could throw themselves enthusiastically into Rosemary's plans. Rosemary tried on short dresses and long dresses, plain dresses and fancy dresses, puritanical dresses with necklines to the chin, and bare-shouldered dresses.

Finally, she compromised. A long dress, with a low neckline and short sleeves. Not too fancy, but a bit of lace. A train, but not a long one.

Then Susan started on the negligees. One for the first night—pure white, but sexy. Two others, colored, but even sexier. Then there were shoes, a headpiece, a going-away dress, and on and on and on. Rosemary felt like a princess.

****

On the morning of his wedding day, Jordan watched Rosemary and Trevor through the dining-room window. They sat outside, at right angles to him, in the old-fashioned porch swing, the one where he had briefly plunked Trevor that first day when he had brought them home.

It was hard to believe that it had been only a little over three months since then. Three months. They'd turned his world upside-down in that short time—for the better. Four months ago, he had not known of Trevor's existence. Now the baby had become the most important person in his world.

No doubt about it, this woman he would soon take as his wife was the second. He wished he'd had the nerve to propose a real marriage to her, but that wouldn't have been fair. That would have been extortion—telling her that if she wanted Trevor she had to take him too.

She was still in her robe, a satin one of peacock blue. In the morning sun, her hair, hanging loose on her shoulders, shone like fine-spun gold.

Trevor sat on her lap. The two heads, one gold, one brown, bent over a Mother Goose picture book.

Rosemary was reading aloud. Jordan watched the two of them in profile. He couldn't hear the words through the window, but he could see the movement of Rosemary's sweet lips, her finger pointing to the words and pictures, and, occasionally, even with the glass barrier, he could hear Trevor's high-pitched giggle.

He cursed under his breath as he watched. A husband in name only, he had promised her. A bit like waving a Christmas dinner under a man's nose and expecting him to say no thanks, he preferred macaroni and cheese. But what choice did he have?

At eight in the morning, the sun already rode high in a cloudless blue sky. *Happy is the bride the sun shines on.* He'd give up half his ranch if he could guarantee that for Rosemary. But he couldn't. The most he could do was be kind to her in small ways to reward her for committing herself to a loveless marriage for the next few years of her life, or however long it took.

The kind thing would have been to beat down his selfish proposal and let her go back to Winnipeg. Trevor was not her child. Gradually her pain would have subsided, she'd have met an unmarried man, fallen in love, had her own family. He'd have depended on lawyers and PI's for Trevor's safety.

Too late now.

At nine Susan would arrive to help Rosemary dress and Debbie would pick up Trevor. Jordan, Rosemary, and Susan would concentrate on getting ready for the eleven o'clock ceremony. Lois and her crew would decorate the house and put the finishing touches on the food.

Jordan watched Rosemary smile and lift her face to the morning sun. Trevor scrambled up and stood on her lap, patting her cheeks with his baby hands. Jordan went into the kitchen, poured two mugs of coffee, and joined them. "Hi."

Rosemary looked up at the sound of his voice. Trevor broke off his patting and held his arms out to Jordan. "Da-dee," he roared. "Da-dee."

"Here." Jordan set one of the mugs on the floor next to Rosemary and sat down beside her, then spoke his thought aloud. "Happy is the bride the sun shines on."

"Da-dee. Da-dee. Da-dee." Trevor bounced against Rosemary's arms, trying to get to Jordan. The leather soles of his baby shoes slipped against the smooth satin of Rosemary's robe, and one section of the robe fell to the side, giving Jordan a more expansive view of long tanned leg than he could handle.

He swallowed and looked away. How the hell was he going to manage living with her? Neither of them had yet brought up the subject of rooms and beds.

Later. He'd worry about that later. He set his mug down and held out his arms to Trevor. "Here, I'll take him." Trevor jumped into Jordan's arms. Rosemary picked up her own cup and took careful sips of coffee, looking straight ahead.

"Nervous?"

She shook her head. "I don't think so. Not really. Everything is so—so taken care of, I guess is what I mean."

He reached out, captured her hand, and held it. She sat quiet as he massaged the back of her hand with his thumb, pausing as he ran it over the solitaire diamond he had given her.

He cleared his throat. "I'll be good to you."

"I know you will." She squeezed the two fingers that lay curled within her hand. "You already have been. You're not going to change the minute we say 'I do.'"

"I know. But still it seems unfair. You should have had a real marriage with real love and a real honeymoon."

Maybe she would say the words now, say that she desired these things with him. Instead she said, "No.

That's all right. Trevor's more important."

She reached out and patted the baby's back, avoiding Jordan's eyes. "There's nothing much to be nervous about, I guess. Not a lot at stake. It's not as if we loved each other."

"No." He raised her hand and kissed the palm before he released it. "It's not as if we loved each other. I'm very grateful to you."

****

Grateful?

Rosemary stared into the mirror at Susan standing behind her.

Jordan had said he was grateful. Not really the words a bride wanted to hear on her wedding day. *Grateful* was how she felt about Susan and Lois. It wasn't how she wanted a new husband to feel about her.

"Sure be good to get you out of that bunk bed and into the bed where you belong." Susan eased the long skirt of the wedding dress over Rosemary's head.

If Susan only knew.

Where was she going to sleep? Rosemary and Jordan had never discussed it.

She fixed her eyes on the reflection of her dress as Susan began to work on the long row of buttons down the back. The dress was lovely—exactly as she'd visualized whenever she'd fantasized about the day she'd marry.

Three rows of lace ribbons framed the neckline and formed the short sleeves. The overskirt had inserts of the same lace, and fell over an underskirt of satin. A chapel-length train, also lace-trimmed, flowed from the waist. She wore no jewels other than a pearl-encrusted headpiece which anchored the elbow-length veil falling down her back, mingling with her ash-blond hair.

Even to herself, this morning she was beautiful.

But where was she going to sleep? She couldn't go on sharing Trevor's room. He was getting older and more talkative every day. Maybe the guest room. With all her clothes left in Jordan's room so Debbie wouldn't guess when she vacuumed twice a week. Sneak in after Trevor was in bed and be out again before he woke up so he wouldn't know either.

Susan patted the veil to make it lie just where it

should.

Rosemary smiled "I suppose Trevor will be all right when I move out. We'll have to leave the bedroom doors open so we can hear if he wakes up. Or put in a baby monitor."

"Mother hen. He's almost two. Fussy toddlers usually survive. Ask Lois about it. She's had four."

"Trevor's not fussy."

"If you say so. Now, let's have a look at you." She stood back, one finger tapping her chin. "Aha. Very nice."

Susan's own ice-green dress was cut in a similar style to Rosemary's, but without the lace, the train, or the veil, and it was short, falling just below the knees.

The doorbell rang. Susan disappeared and soon returned with two bouquets. "Our flowers." She backed through the door, leaving it open. She laid the two bouquets, one white, one yellow, on the top bunk.

"Roses. Roses for the rancher's Rose. I got yellow ones for you. White ones for me. I thought about red ones, but they're so common." She patted her French roll proudly. "Besides, they clash with my hair, even if you're the one wearing them."

Rosemary reached out and hugged her. "Susan, you're a nut. And I love you."

A sudden silence fell. They heard Jordan whistling in the big bedroom.

"Hmm…" Susan winked. "Groom sounds happy. Thinking about tonight, I'll bet. Guess there's something to be said for making them wait. You did make him wait?"

Rosemary thought of how they'd fought to avoid physical contact ever since they'd decided to marry. She concentrated on framing the lie. Sometimes she wished she didn't have quite so much in common with the ten-year-old George Washington.

"Well, I guess maybe he made me wait."

"It'll be worth it. You'll see."

"So where are Jordan and I going?" Rosemary asked.

"That's for me to know and you to find out."

"We'll have to find out if we're going there."

"You'll find out." Susan reached out and tweaked the veil "It's in with the wedding presents. It's a small wedding, so you'll open them at the reception."

Rosemary sighed with mock exasperation. "Anything you two haven't thought of?"

Susan shook her head. "Not a thing. We talked about getting you something for birth control, but then decided Jordan will probably worry about that. Besides, we thought maybe you wanted babies instead."

Rosemary sat silent.

"That last bit was a joke." Susan wrinkled her nose and chuckled. "The part about the hotel reservation being in the gifts wasn't though."

Melodies of love songs drifted down the hall. Rosemary listened. "Music?"

"That's Belinda," Susan said. "She's in charge of the sound system. That means 'Here Comes the Bride' will start in fifteen minutes. You're ready?"

Rosemary nodded and sat down on the chair in front of the window, arranging her skirt carefully around her so as not to crease it. She heard Jordan's steps as he moved through the hall in front of his bedroom.

"You've got his ring?"

Susan nodded. "Of course I have. That's what bridesmaids are for."

The music changed. Susan picked up her own bouquet of white roses and started for the door. "Good luck, friend." She turned back and kissed Rosemary. "You're marrying a wonderful guy."

Rosemary stepped out to see her father in the doorway. "Hi, Daddy. Sorry we didn't have you staying here, but Lois decided against it."

"It's okay." He squeezed her hand and chuckled. "She knew you were busy. Anyway, we've had a great time. Lois's parents just sort of took us over. We're going to spend the weekend in Jasper National Park with them. Her dad and I have spent a lot of time talking shop. Sorry we haven't got to know Jordan better, but what we've seen, we like. Let's go, honey." He added, "I hope you don't find starting married life with a child too difficult."

She touched his cheek and smiled. "It won't be a problem. I love Trevor. You know that." At least she'd sidestepped any questions about whether she loved Jordan.

She rested her palm on her father's arm and walked

beside him through the halls of the bedroom wing, through the family room, past Belinda and the stereo controls, and out to the big patio at the back of the house.

Rosemary blinked. Lois and her crew had been busy. Rows of folding chairs filled the patio, and most of the chairs were occupied. Every ranch family for twenty miles around must have turned up.

Rosemary walked past the neighbors she hadn't met, the neighbors she had met, and the few close friends and family at the front.

Rosemary's mother sat in the front row, an empty seat beside her, and next to that were four chairs for Ken and Debbie and the two toddlers. Right now, they were all standing, Ken holding Trevor high so he could see.

Trevor held out his arms. "Aunty Wose. Aunty Wose. Aunty Wose."

Rosemary paused and kissed him, then whispered in his ear, "Be a good boy, Trevor."

The guests smiled and chuckled. Rosemary heard the murmurs from behind her. "How sweet." "Isn't she beautiful?" "What an adorable little boy!"

Then there was Jordan. She caught her breath. He was so handsome, in his dark suit, gleaming white shirt, black oxfords polished until they shone. The muted whirr of a video camera sounded in the background.

"Who gives this woman to this man?" Lois's second cousin from Calgary asked, and Rosemary's dad replied, "Her mother and I do." Then he sat down and all attention focused on Rosemary and Jordan.

Jordan smiled down on her and squeezed her hand. He spoke his responses in a firm clear tone. She was confident he meant most of them. He would care for her in sickness and in health. At least for a year or so. He promised here, before this congregation, that he would worship her with his body. He had promised in private that he wouldn't.

Why should the thought of facing celibacy for part of her youth bother her? He was doing the same. He would never be unfaithful. It wasn't in his character.

He could never love her, he had said. That didn't really matter, did it? She didn't love him either, she told herself firmly. But in her twenty-eight years of life she

133

hadn't found anyone else she loved. Many of her friends who protested undying love had really married just for the sake of being married—not nearly as good a reason as mutual love of a child. Some of these friends were on their second and third marriages based on eternal love.

It would be all right. Time to convince this new world of hers. She smiled at Jordan as he put the wedding band on her ring finger, and, when the time came, raised her face eagerly for his kiss.

His lips came down on hers, firm and mobile. Yes, and hungry. Her life force drained from her body, from her lips into his, almost as if she and Jordan were already merging into one person. She raised one hand to cup the back of his head. He responded by tightening his grasp around her waist, pulling her against his hard body. She'd have collapsed if he had not held her up.

When it was over, she knew in her mind that the kiss had lasted only a few chaste seconds. Her body said it had gone on for hours. Perhaps Jordan had more than a bit of the actor in him too.

With luck, the hotel room would have two beds.

****

After the ceremony, Jordan stood beside Rosemary in the receiving line, shaking hands with his friends and neighbors, introducing Rosemary to the ones who didn't already know her.

Behind them sounded a cacophony of chairs scraping the floor, and folding tables crashing into upright positions. Lois and half a dozen helpers trotted back and forth carrying salads and casseroles to place on two of the tables, along with cutlery, paper plates, and flowers.

Jordan looked down on his bride. She was beautiful. She stood, turned slightly toward him, her left hand resting like a feather upon his arm as she smiled and laughed, shook hands with everyone, kissed the women she had come to know. Belinda's love songs once more played in the background, but softly, so as not to interfere with conversation. A beautiful wedding. Very unlike his first one, a hurried affair in a registry office because Blair wasn't interested in meeting his friends and neighbors.

He shook hands automatically, and conversed with guests, including Rosemary in conversations with the old friends she had not met until today. After the last person passed through the receiving line, Rosemary squeezed Jordan's arm and smiled up at him. Without thinking, he bent his head and kissed her gently on the cheek. She smiled again, and caressed his face. He hadn't known he had tears in his eyes just looking at her, until he felt her thumb below his eye, brushing one of them away.

"We'd better get the reception started," she said. "I understand we're expected to sit down before anyone else can."

The rituals went by. Len Peterson gave the toast to the bride, and Jordan listened, his heart full. He'd known Rosemary only a few months, Len said. In that length of time, she'd made her way into their hearts with her selfless care of Trevor, her friendliness, her instant acceptance of ranch life. Jordan agreed. Rosemary was the most unselfish woman he'd ever met, and he was lucky enough to have her for his wife.

He felt a blinding flash of hatred for Blair, the woman who had treated him in such a way that he had become incapable of expressing his love. He vowed love or no love, to show Rosemary such caring and appreciation that she would never have cause to regret what she had done.

The toast ended. Jordan responded, choosing his words carefully, expressing his gratitude to Rosemary, to the community that had taken her to their hearts, to Lois and Susan for planning and making this beautiful wedding for the two of them. This was what friends and neighbors were all about.

The reception went on—the toasts, the visiting, the cake cutting, and, interspersed with increasing frequency, the tapping of spoons against glasses, the signal that the bride and groom were to get to their feet and kiss.

It was a nice custom, Jordan thought. They could tap their glasses every thirty seconds if they wanted. He had no objection to standing, bending his head, touching his lips to Rosemary's, feeling the velvet of her skin, taking in the fresh scent of her perfume, feeling her hair against his fingers. If only it didn't have to end there…

Last came the opening of the gifts. Lois brought Rosemary a stack of envelopes. "We got together and decided what you needed. What you didn't need were dishes and cutlery and plastic swans to hold extra rolls of toilet paper. We knew you had all that stuff. So we got you gift certificates."

Rosemary and Jordan began on the envelopes. Gift certificates from a china shop. Gift certificates from a department store. Jordan looked down at his new wife. Tears glistened on her cheeks as she opened envelope after envelope. A tack shop—a gift certificate so that Rosemary could buy her own saddle. Several neighbors had shared this one—saddles weren't cheap.

One from a riding academy for a series of riding lessons. Several from restaurants in the area for dining out. From Debbie, who still didn't have a lot of cash, four days of free baby-sitting, starting immediately. Finally, the one Lois handed them last, three nights in a posh Calgary hotel, everything included.

Rosemary gestured helplessly toward the guests. "Thank you. Thank you so much. For taking me into your lives and your hearts. For giving us this wedding when our original plans were a justice of the peace and dinner out before we came back home. Thank you for giving me riding lessons instead of plastic swans—"

Her voice broke. Jordan picked up his napkin and swabbed her eyes, then held her close. "Thanks again, folks. Sorry I've been out of circulation so long. I think today marks the beginning not only of my new life with my beautiful bride, but my reentry into the life of this community."

****

A group of hopeful teen-age girls gathered on the lawn below the patio as Rosemary prepared to throw her bouquet. First, she broke off a single yellow rose and tucked it into her hair, wedging it under the tiara.

Lois's daughter Belinda caught the bouquet. Everyone laughed when Lois muttered, "Not for at least another eight years, you aren't."

Next came the ritual of the garter. Young men and teen-age boys replaced the girls. Rosemary turned her back on Jordan, laughing and hiking up her skirts. He hunkered behind her to the accompaniment of cheers and clapping. He clasped Rosemary around the ankle. She put her weight on the other leg and grasped the patio railing for support. Jordan slid his hands up her leg, slowly, sensuously. The way their audience wanted.

I'm going to attack the man. If this goes on another minute, I'm going to pounce on him and have my way with him right here and now in front of all these people. This was not the proper beginning for a platonic marriage. Rosemary tried to concentrate on the garter and its meaning, tried to hold back her gasps of pleasure as Jordan's hands traveled slowly up her leg. This garter was both her something blue and her something borrowed—from Susan. Chuck had caught it when Len and Lois married.

Rosemary treasured her place on this chain of continuity—being part of a community where the same traditions, the same people, went on and on. She might well preside at the tea table when Belinda married, and Belinda might well be organist at Trevor's wedding. After all, Jordan had promised her a continued part in Trevor's life.

Jordan's hands passed her knee, inched halfway up her thigh, and grasped the garter. No amount of determined contemplation could keep Rosemary's thoughts from Jordan. She closed her eyes and held her breath, following each tiny movement of the garter down her leg with fantasies of the coming night.

Then it was over. Jordan threw the garter. A young cowboy from the ranch past Peterson's caught it. Rosemary released her pent-up breath, and turned to Jordan.

An hour of kissing and gossip and picture taking followed. Everybody had cameras. "Would the bride and groom pose please?" "Here, Chuck, take a picture of me with Rosemary." "Please, Rosemary, could you pose for Belinda."

From Rosemary's mother, "A couple quick snaps of you and Jordan, dear. I know you'll send me copies of the video and other pictures, but I want one right away for the Winnipeg paper."

Then, as if on a signal, families picked up their empty casserole dishes and faded away. Except for Ken and Debbie, the only ones remaining were a clean-up crew, consisting of Susan, Lois, and half a dozen teenagers. Then Ken and Debbie left, still carrying Trevor, allowing him a kiss and cuddle from Jordan and Rosemary.

"I'll take good care of Trevor," Debbie promised as she hugged Rosemary. "And Ken will take good care of the ranch. We'll keep an eye on the house for you too. Have a wonderful time."

They disappeared, Ken carrying his own son, Trevor looking back over Debbie's shoulder, waving and calling, "Bye-bye, Da-dee. Bye-bye, Aunty Wose. Bye-bye."

"Isn't he beautiful?" Rosemary said as she watched them leave.

"So are you," Jordan said, his voice husky.

Rosemary started down the hall toward Trevor's room.

Jordan put an arm around her and guided her into his room. "Huh uh. Our public image, remember. The clean-up crew is still around. A real new bride would come in here."

Timely reminder. Just in case she'd begun to think of herself as a truly married woman. She turned away and focused her attention on a fresh-picked vase of poppies, in every color of the rainbow, which stood on the dresser. Rosemary traced the velvet petals of one with a forefinger.

Jordan smiled. "Another touch from Lois and her crew."

"Oh! Aren't they—I mean—"

"Yes." Jordan cupped her chin in his hand. "They are. Lois and the flowers both. Now don't start crying on me. Turn around, and I'll undo your buttons for you."

"You're lucky." Rosemary turned her back to him. "In the old days they had about two-hundred of them."

Jordan chuckled. "That wouldn't be so bad. Spin out the suspense." He undid the row of buttons—down her back, past her waist, past her hips, letting his fingers caress the expanse of smooth skin between the bra and the crinoline. Jordan eased the dress from her shoulders and over her hips, taking his time, letting his palms linger on every inch, letting his lips touch the nape of her neck when he straightened up.

"Okay. Step out of it," he said.

She stepped out of the dress and stood before him in her bra, crinoline, and panty hose.

He eyed the crinoline. "Down or up?"

"Down, I think."

The crinoline followed the path of the dress. He picked them up from the carpet and tossed them onto the bed.

In the distance they could hear the slamming of car doors, indicating that the cleaning crew was leaving.

She could feel his gaze on her skin as she stood there in her bra and pantyhose. "You're beautiful." He ran his tongue around the edge of his lips, then looked away. "I'll fetch some jeans and a shirt for you."

"Jeans? What about my going-away suit?"

"You can put that on in the city. Might as well be comfortable."

"Of course."

After all, once the audience had left, this was just a day like any other.

Chapter Eleven

Rosemary watched as Jordan opened the door to their hotel room, then stood back for her to precede him.

Fresh flowers filled the room. Thousands of them, it seemed. Daisies and roses, tulips and gladioli, carnations and lilies, orange blossoms and forget-me-nots.

Rosemary examined a large mixed bouquet on the dresser. "There's a card. From Len and Lois. The hotel didn't supply these flowers. They're from our friends."

Jordan stood beside her, and pushed aside a daisy that covered a corner of the card. "Have a great three days," he read aloud. "Love, Len and Lois." He echoed Rosemary's words. "From our friends."

Two dozen red roses graced the headboard of the bed. From the middle of the vase, three black-eyed Susans winked. Rosemary closed her eyes and buried her nose in the roses, inhaling the scent for a few seconds before beginning to read. "From Chuck and Susan. If that man doesn't have you..." She broke off and read the rest silently with Jordan peering over her shoulder, "...pregnant by morning, it better not be for want of trying, or he'll have me to answer to. Love, Susan. P.S. Red roses are for love, but don't you think those other posies add an elegant touch?"

Jordan chuckled.

A little clump of carnations stood in a round glass bowl on the chest of drawers. Rosemary read the card, then turned to Jordan, a lump in her throat and tears in her eyes. "It's from Ken and Debbie. And from Trevor. It says, 'Yes, I know these are Mother's Day flowers, but Trevor says you're the most wonderful mother a kid could ever have. At least, he'd say that if he knew how. Love, Ken, Debbie, Dennis, and Trevor.' Oh, Jordan, they don't have any money—just the little we've already paid them, and they sent us flowers."

Jordan took her face in his hands and, with his

thumbs, brushed away the two tears that rolled down her cheek. Then he touched his forehead to hers. "I think we'd better get ready for dinner. You change here. I'll take the bathroom." He released her, and patted her behind. "I'll just get my suit out of the garment bag. How long do you need?"

"Twenty minutes? But I want a quick shower first."

"All right. You have your shower. Then when you're finished, we'll trade places."

As soon as Rosemary returned, he left, one finger hooked into the hanger holding the suit he had worn for the wedding. She could hear him whistling the "The Red River Valley."

Rosemary's canary-yellow suit featured a classic jacket and a short smart skirt. She took the yellow rose she had saved from her bridal bouquet, and fastened it to the lapel, then dressed. With the suit, she wore a royal-blue silk blouse, which her friends had agreed brought out the blue in her smoke-colored eyes. While she waited for Jordan, she inventoried the room. One queen-size bed. One triple dresser. One queen-size bed. One tall chest of drawers. One queen-size bed. A million or so flowers. One queen-size bed. Two dressers, a million flowers, but only one bed. No couches, no sofa beds. She could hardly ask Jordan to sleep in the bathtub.

Then there were the negligees, three of them. One for each night. Susan had insisted on helping her pack, so she couldn't sneak in any of her modest over-sized tee shirts. She was stuck with the negligees, each one sexier than the one before. It was either those or sleep in her blue jeans. She had nothing in between. She'd have to be sure to be in bed, sheets pulled up around her chin, before he saw her.

At dinner, she sat in the posh restaurant and pushed the expensive food around her plate.

"The steak's very good," Jordan said.

Rosemary dutifully nibbled a tiny piece. "Yes, it's excellent, isn't it?"

"Potatoes are done nicely."

"Yes, very nicely. So are the carrots."

"Yes, they are. I wonder if the restaurant bakes their own bread."

Oh, hell. She threw down her cutlery and glowered at him across the table. She looked around the room to make sure the other diners were all strangers.

"We haven't talked about anything," she said, keeping her voice low. "I don't even know where I'm going to sleep when we get home."

Jordan calmly cut another piece of steak. "Wherever you'd like, I guess."

"Well, I can't keep sleeping in the same room as Trevor. In a few more months he's going to be old enough to notice everything and talk well enough to share what he knows with the whole world."

"All right. He should probably start getting used to sleeping by himself anyway."

"That leaves my study and the guestroom. I like to think of my study as the place where I work." She glared at him. "If you were a businessman, how'd you like to sleep in your office?"

He raised his hands in a conciliatory gesture. "Fine. Don't sleep in the study."

"That just leaves the guestroom. What if we have guests?"

"How many guests have we had so far?"

She ignored his question. "Anyway, whatever I do, I'll have to leave all my clothes in your room, and sneak somewhere else to sleep, and get up again before Trevor wakes up so he won't see me leaving—wherever. I'll have to leave the room looking unused, so Debbie won't catch on when she cleans the house."

Damn Jordan anyway. He chose this moment to look amused, as if she were an unreasonable child. After all, *he* was the one who'd established the guidelines. He could at least pretend take an interest. Finally, he looked at her. "That's all up to you, I guess," he said. "Where are you planning to sleep tonight?"

****

Jordan opened the door of the hotel room, and put his hand gently on Rosemary's back to let her precede him.

What was he supposed to say? He'd probably been rude with his refusal to discuss anything and his question about where she'd sleep tonight, and he hated himself for it. But damn it all, after the wedding, the kisses, the

142

warmth he'd felt from her when he'd removed the garter—could she blame him for thinking that maybe she'd changed her mind? For hoping that tonight they'd both crawl into that queen-size bed and let nature take its course?

Sure, the platonic thing had been his idea—well, the lawyer's idea really, but he'd gone along with it. Mostly because he was afraid she'd turn down a real proposal. The marriage of convenience had been the right thing to do, but, privately, he'd hoped she'd ask to change the guidelines. Ha! His lustful thoughts had been slapped down in short order. Her behavior at the wedding and reception had been part of her act.

He tossed his suit jacket onto the bed and loosened his tie. Then he picked up the remote and sat in the easy chair. "Might catch the end of the Edmonton-Saskatchewan game."

Rosemary fidgeted in the middle of the room. Her eyes kept darting toward the bed. Jordan found himself ignoring the green and white uniforms on the TV and stared at the bed himself. Only one bed there. It dominated the room with its pink bedspread and fluffy pillows. It taunted and winked and grew till the damned bed appeared to be the only thing in the room. Rosemary was looking at the thing as if it were a poisonous snake.

"It's all right." Jordan flicked off the TV. "I'll take the bathtub."

"The bathtub? You don't have to do that."

"Any other suggestions?"

"It's a big bed." She dragged her view from the bed and looked at him. "I guess if you take one side, I can take the other."

"All right." He stood. "I'll go change in the bathroom again, and you can change out here and get into bed. Ten minutes?"

****

After the bathroom door closed behind Jordan, Rosemary took a froth of white silk and lace from the garment bag. This wasn't the thing to wear tonight, but the other two were worse. The luxurious material caressed her face when she held it against her. She undressed, putting her suit and blouse onto a hanger,

143

folding her underclothes neatly before she put them in a dresser drawer. Then she slipped into the negligee.

She posed before the mirror, then whistled softly at her own image. The gown hung straight and sleek, almost to the floor, held up by thin spaghetti straps. Her pink bare toes peeked out below it. The sheer silk revealed the outline of her body. The low-cut lace top showcased everything it pretended to conceal.

The bathroom door clicked, and she spun around. Jordan stood self-consciously in the doorway, wearing blue and white striped sleep pants which still held the creases of the packaging. She suspected he didn't wear any when on his own. His chest was as bare as it had been the night he'd removed his shirt to dry her tears.

"Oh," he said. "Sorry. You said ten minutes." He stopped, then looked at her as if he'd never seen her before. "My God!"

Slowly, he walked toward her. She stood rooted where she was, spellbound, her eyes focused on his dark chest hair and the spot where it tapered off into the sleep pants. When he reached her, he put out one hand and stroked her cheek. "Rosemary."

She could only stare at him, unmoving. He caressed the side of her neck, pausing on the pounding pulse.

"Rosemary. Darling." His voice thickened with emotion. She held her breath. His caresses moved downward, rotating around her shoulder, easing along the arm, finally teasing the side of her breast. Her held breath disappeared with a whoosh. Jordan still gazed down at her, fondled her breast. She flung herself against him, tangling her hands in his hair and lifted her face to him.

His mouth raided hers, and she forgot everything— the marriage of convenience, the conversation about sleeping arrangements, the careful orchestration of who dressed where when. His lips crushed hers, and his wiry chest hair chafed her breasts through the flimsy lace top.

He ran his tongue around the inside of her lips, then stroked the ridges on the top of her mouth.

She came unhinged.

Jordan grasped the spaghetti straps and eased them over her shoulders, then nudged the lace top of her negligee downward, leaving nothing between his chest and the delicate skin of her breasts. Nothing but his hands, stroking, massaging, inflaming.

He removed his mouth from hers. "Please, Rosemary," he pleaded. "Please, darling."

Existence stopped for her. Her brain, her heart, her very being all gave in to raw lustful feeling. All that remained was the sensation in her breasts and the throbbing pulse of her desire. After all, she was married to the man. "Yes," she whispered. "Oh, yes."

He lifted her in his arms and took the two short steps to the bed, pulled back the satin cover, then fell on the sheets with her, the two of them entangled.

"Let's get rid of this thing," he said as he grasped the hem of the negligee. On his way to getting rid of it, he massaged her ankles, her legs, her knees, her thighs. A wave of heat followed his hands. When he reached her waist, he stroked her stomach. The flimsy silk of the negligee lay draped across his lower arms.

Onward and upward, over her rib cage, over her breasts. She moaned and bit her lower lip, not touching him, willing herself to do nothing that might interfere with the magic of his hands. When the garment lay draped above her breasts, she lifted her arms. He slipped the negligee over her head and tossed it to the floor. Then he propped himself on one elbow, and gazed upon her.

"You're beautiful," he said. "So beautiful. I—I want you so badly."

He shed the sleep pants.

Rosemary wound her arms around his neck, her body pressed against him.

"Rosemary, darling." Again he caressed her breasts, stroked her stomach, ran his hands over her legs.

When she was flushed and quivering with unbearable desire, the promise of the wedding kiss was at last fulfilled, and Rosemary knew that she and Jordan were merged forever, that they were now and for eternity one person.

She let out her held breath and gave herself to pleasing him.

****

Jordan came half-awake to find Rosemary curled

against him. Was he dreaming? He'd dreamed this scene often enough—Rosemary in his bed, and something wonderful happening between them.

He blinked, and took a moment to orient himself. It all came back. The something wonderful, in the cold light of morning, had become something shameful. Jordan Sterling, the man who prided himself on never going back on his word, had done exactly that, and had betrayed the most beautiful and wonderful woman in the world.

He heard Rosemary murmur to herself, then move. He made himself look toward her. Her golden hair lay spread against the pillow. Her skin glowed. She smiled at him. He forced himself to smile back. "I'm sorry, Rosemary. I acted like an animal. It won't happen again. I promise."

Her smile disappeared, and her face closed against him. "I see," she said. And then, "It's all right."

He put his hand over hers. "No, honey. It's not all right. I made a promise to you, and I broke it." He paused. "Now, why don't you have a shower, and when you're dressed we'll go down to breakfast and talk about what's happened?"

****

Rosemary reached down and grasped the fallen negligee. She wrapped it around her like a giant bandage, and stumbled to the bathroom. She stood in front of the vanity, leaning against it, the negligee trapped between her body and the edge.

It's all right, she had told Jordan.

Last night, when she lay in his arms, she'd thought it was all right. Last night, when she suddenly realized she loved this man she was married to she had thought he loved her too.

He didn't.

She moved away from the vanity. The negligee dropped in a heap at her feet. She ignored it as she crossed to the shower and turned on the taps. The needles of hot water drummed against her skin. She lingered, staying and staying and staying. Delaying the moment that she must leave this sanctuary and once again face Jordan, to decide, in a civilized manner of course, what they were going to do.

146

Finally, she turned off the taps, dried herself, and wrapped the largest towel around her, tucking the ends in securely so that she was as completely shrouded as if inside a cocoon.

She scurried into the bedroom, and before Jordan had time to blink, snatched up underclothes, jeans, and a shirt, then scurried back.

When she returned, dressed but barefoot, Jordan was sitting in the large chair, complete with jeans, shirt, and cowboy boots. Rosemary perched on the edge of the bed and gazed at the spot where the ceiling met the far wall. The silence spun out, taut as a newly tuned guitar string.

"So what next?" Jordan asked a little while later over breakfast. "We have two more days in this hotel. Do you want to play tourist, or what?"

"No." Rosemary forked a strawberry to her mouth. "I want to go home. I want Trevor. I already miss him.

They ate breakfast in awkward silence. When they returned to the room, Jordan began to take clothes from the closet and pack. Rosemary did the same.

She looked around her and gestured helplessly. "What about the flowers?"

"I suppose we'd better take them."

She shrugged and took each bouquet from its vase, wrapped the stems in damp toilet paper, and bundled them in the plastic bags she'd used to wrap her shoes.

"All right, I'm ready." She picked up the flowers and her overnight bag and marched to the door. Jordan followed her, suitcases in hand.

What, she wondered, would be the next step.

****

The rain started just as Rosemary and Jordan drove across the cattle guard at the beginning of the driveway. Clouds had moved in soon after they left Calgary. Now fat drops of rain splashed on the windshield. A cold finger of depression stroked Rosemary's back. She shivered.

Jordan smiled sardonically. "Happy homecoming."

"It doesn't matter." She tried to smile. "The pastures probably need the rain."

By time Debbie met them at her front door, Rosemary had shifted into her college actress mode. "I'm so glad to be home." She knew she was overdoing it. "We

147

had a wonderful time, but we came home early because we missed Trevor so much. We couldn't bear to be away from him a minute longer." She smiled over her shoulder at Jordan. "Right, honey?"

Jordan jingled his keys. "That's right, sweetheart."

Trevor scrambled around Debbie's legs and out the door. "Da-Dee, Auntie Wose. Da-Dee. Auntie Wose." He launched himself into Jordan's arms. The reunion, thankfully, took the pressure off the need for make believe. At least for now.

Rosemary and Debbie hugged. "Thanks for everything." Rosemary pressed her cheek briefly against Debbie's. "We'd better get Trevor home now."

"Yes," Debbie agreed. "It's almost time for his morning sleep."

Jordan and Rosemary darted the few feet to the car through the rain, and dived for the shelter of the vehicle. Thankfully, they could enter their own house through the attached garage.

"I'll put Trevor down for his nap."

"All right." Rosemary began gathering up the bouquets. "I'll do something with these flowers."

Thank goodness Jordan was with Trevor. He couldn't witness the quivering of her chin nor the tears that gathered in her eyes as she laid the bags of flowers gently in one side of the stainless steel sink while she rummaged for vases. All she'd could think about was escaping from the shabby memories—memories that should have been the most beautiful ones of her life. The red roses from Susan had already begun to wilt. Rosemary couldn't hold back the tears that dropped on the petals. Why did the most beautiful things have the shortest life spans?

She removed the damp paper towel from the stems, and rescued the black-eyed Susans to put with the poppies Lois had left on their dresser. She placed the roses in the compost pail. When the first bouquets were in containers, she unwrapped the rest and painstakingly arranged them, then placed them around the family room and living room.

The last was the inexpensive arrangement of carnations from Debbie and Ken. Their monetary value was small, but the love that had gone into choosing them had been immense. Rosemary stood in front of the sink holding the flowers, tears streaming down her cheeks, when she heard Jordan's footsteps. He'd have changed into an old shirt and worn jeans. He'd be even sexier in those. Her heart ached, but she daren't turn around. She picked up the little jar of carnations and took them into her study. She wouldn't share these flowers with Jordan. Carnations were for mothers, and she was the only mother Trevor would ever have.

She continued on to the family room, flopped down in her recliner, and stared into the cold ashes of the fire. Jordan appeared a few minutes later, carrying two mugs of steaming coffee. She accepted one gratefully, thankful for the warmth and cheer it brought into this cheerless day. While she sipped, she looked at Jordan. This discussion was his idea. He could go first.

Finally he spoke. "Well?"

"Well, what?"

"Where do you want to sleep?"

She paused and thought. "I guess I'd better sleep in the big bed in the master bedroom."

He choked on his coffee. "So where do you want me to sleep?"

"Same place, I guess."

"You're serious?"

"Very much so. Think about it, Jordan. In the eyes of the community we're happily married. If I keep sleeping where I've been, Trevor will spill the beans before long. He's getting more talkative every day. Even if I take the guest room, sooner or later somebody will catch on. Will I have every last trace of being there removed before Debbie cleans? Trevor will wake up in the night and not be able to find me." She paused. "To say nothing of the social workers who keep traipsing through, analyzing the sort of home environment we're providing."

"Yeah. I suppose you're right." He stood up. "Okay, I'll take the suitcases in there. I won't break my word again, but it'd sure make it easier if you'd start wearing something really ugly to bed instead of that thing you had on last night."

****

That evening, Rosemary sat in the family room,

pretending to watch television while Jordan went out to the barn. What else was new? When he returned he marched straight through into the bedroom wing. Going to be asleep before she got there, she presumed. Good. She watched the early news, two game shows, a special on the conditioning of white rats, and finally the late evening news.

Nothing more for it. She had to traipse off into that bedroom.

Sure enough, Jordan was curled up on one side of the bed with his back to the middle. Rosemary snorted silently. She could play his game.

Quietly, she undressed and slipped into her ugliest sleep shirt. It was an old one, left over from her teenaged years, that she'd grabbed in her haste when leaving her apartment. It was faded purple with an equally faded green and red dragon on the front. She slipped into bed beside Jordan and turned her back to him, being careful to leave a full eighteen inches of space between them.

Eventually, she slept fitfully, only to be awakened by a voice from the hall.

"Aunty Wose. Aunty Wose." Trevor had awakened and realized she wasn't there in the top bunk.

She sat up in bed. "In here, baby. Come on in."

Trevor pattered in on baby feet, and she pulled him into bed with her.

"Uh." Jordan struggled into wakefulness. "Wha's going on?"

"It's Trevor. He woke up and missed me." She lifted Trevor over, into the space between them.

"Daddy. Aunty Wose. Daddy." He snuggled down between them, totally content.

A real family. Just like a real family. Rosemary prayed a little prayer that Trevor would never discover the difference. She'd made the right decision to sleep in the big bed with Jordan. After all, Trevor was what this marriage was all about, and if it meant sharing a loveless bed with Jordan and having social workers traipsing through the house, so be it.

****

The next hurdle, the most difficult, was the play group. Lois and Susan, especially Susan, would be a lot

150

harder to fool than Ken and Debbie. She couldn't put it off, though. The longer she did that, the more suspicious they might become.

By the time of the play group, the rainy days had gone away, succeeded by the brilliant sun of the Rockies. The deck was a lovely place to spend the afternoon. Rosemary brought out all of Trevor's blocks and farm toys, as well as the coffee cups, brownies, and coffee pot.

She was already sitting on the deck when Lois and Susan and their toddlers arrived. Debbie walked over with Dennis a few minutes later. The toddlers raced for Trevor's toys while the women hugged and kissed.

Susan spread her hands. "Now, pour us some coffee and then tell us all about your honeymoon."

I don't think so. She glanced at the four children. They played quietly at the other end of the deck—Trevor with Tinker Bell's Barbie Camper, the other three with Trevor's tractors. She poured coffee and gestured to the brownies on a low table.

"Now." Susan cupped her chin in one hand and leaned forward. "Tell all."

"Susan," Lois remonstrated. "Just let her tell us what she wants to."

"That's all right," Rosemary said. She forced another silly smile. "It was wonderful."

Well, she didn't have to lie about everything. Her reaction to the flowers, and even Jordan's reaction. She couldn't keep back the tears as she relived the steps from one bouquet to another, the reading of each card. She wiped her eyes on one of the paper napkins that sat beside the plate of brownies.

"Well, are you?" Susan demanded.

"Am I what?"

"Pregnant. That's what my note said."

Rosemary shook her head. "I don't think so." A wave of terror struck as it suddenly occurred to her that it wouldn't be impossible. And wouldn't that be the cap to this honeymoon from Hell?

She gave her eyes one last wipe and went on. The dinner. How delicious the steak was. The décor of the room. How pretty the negligees were.

And when Susan asked if Jordan had enjoyed

removing the first one, she nodded her head and said, quite honestly, "Oh yes."

****

Jordon wandered into Rosemary's study. The women and kids were out on the deck, and he was at loose ends. Wanting Rosemary, but not being permitted to have her. Lingering here in the room she used was the closest he'd ever get.

The time they spent together in the big bed didn't count. That was a nightly exercise in frustration and self-restraint. He pretended to be asleep when she came in after she watched the evening news. By time she woke up in the morning, he was long gone, out doing the ranch chores. The only happy night had been that first one, when Trevor had wandered in and snuggled down to sleep between them.

He glanced around Rosemary's study—her computer, of course, and the printer she'd bought after she'd come here to replace the one she'd left in Winnipeg. The thing he didn't remember from last time he'd been here was a large dictionary on the dresser, with the pages gapped in the middle. Curious, he opened it. There was a flower there, drying. A single yellow rose. The one she'd picked from her wedding bouquet to wear on the lapel of her suit jacket. It was in a Ziploc bag, probably so it wouldn't stain the pages of the heavy book.

He picked the plastic bag from the dictionary and looked thoughtfully at the flower. Flowers and Rosemary were linked together in his heart, had been from that first delicate whiff of her perfume. He remembered the flowers in the mountain meadow where they'd picnicked, and the bouquet of wildflowers he'd given her one evening. He thought of their wedding—her yellow roses, the bowl of poppies in their bedroom, the hotel room filled with flowers from their friends.

Rosemary's yellow rose didn't belong in a dictionary. He laid the Ziploc bag on the dresser, then went to his room and returned with the album she had given him. The one with her memories of Trevor. He saw a drop of water on the plastic bag and realised he was crying. He dried the bag on his sleeve and slipped it between the pages of the album.

Chapter Twelve

The days at the Sterling ranch established their own pattern as they followed one upon the other. There had been several interviews with social workers. Rosemary had gone through the house with them, trying to make the right impression, hoping to convince them that Jordan had the best of homes, the best of wives, to bring up a child. When they reminded her that a baby's birth mother had the strongest claim, she forced herself to smile calmly and keep to herself her hopes that the private investigator would find something to change that.

In the mornings, she played with Trevor and did domestic things—baking cookies, planning meals, doing laundry. One morning over breakfast, Jordan said abruptly, "Let's go shopping."

"Shopping?"

"Yeah. You know. Shopping. Like in a store buying things. We can use our gift certificates."

"Well." Rosemary wiped cereal from Trevor's chin. "We, uh, really haven't decided what we want, have we? Wine glasses or stick-free pans, or..." She waved her hands helplessly in the air.

Jordan grinned. "I think there's one gift we can agree on. The saddle. So why don't we go to Calgary this morning and pick one out? I've already asked Debbie if she'll keep Trevor all morning and maybe part of the afternoon, if we decide to stay in the city for lunch."

Rosemary gaped at Jordan. She couldn't help it. Was the thaw finally setting in? "Oh. Sure. I'll just clear away the breakfast things." She reached for Jordan's plate. Her hand shook.

"Go get ready," Jordan said. "I'll take care of the clearing up and Trevor."

The store was filled with saddles and bridles and riding boots and Stetsons.

But the gift certificate stipulated a saddle, so

Rosemary ignored everything else. She walked down the long rows of saddles—western saddles, English saddles, tan ones, light brown ones, dark brown ones, black ones, children's saddles, roping saddles. She flipped price tags as she went.

"Get what you want," Jordan said. "If it's more than the amount of the gift certificate, I'll pay the difference."

Rosemary didn't think there'd be a problem. The only ones above the price of the gift certificate were the heavy professional ones used in rodeos.

She turned her attention back to the saddles and narrowed her choices. A clerk put the ones she pointed at on a stand one by one so she could sit on them, try them out.

She finally chose a tan-colored one, light enough she could easily lift it, so she could quit letting Jordan get her horse ready for her.

Her friends had said the saddle was for long idyllic rides. Hah. Up until this morning, she'd assumed that long idyllic rides had gone the way of long idyllic sex— that rides of any kind had gone the way of sex of any kind. If that's still the way it was, maybe she'd throw her new saddle on Molly and ride on her own.

She also had a certificate for riding lessons. So who needed Jordan Sterling anyway? She did, but she wouldn't beg.

Jordan tossed the saddle, along with a new bridle, into the back of the Jeep and drove to a restaurant. He opened the door for her, and Rosemary drew in her breath. It was an upscale restaurant, not a diner, and it wasn't one of the places covered by a gift certificate. The lights were dim and fresh flowers sat in the middle of each table. Had Jordan planned this? Made a reservation? It hadn't been a sudden thought over breakfast, after all. Could he be courting her? Maybe their marriage had taken its first step on the long road to recovery.

****

They arrived home in the middle of the afternoon. Rosemary got out of the Jeep in the garage and turned to go for Trevor. Jordan touched her arm.

"Huh uh," he said. "We're going to the barn."

The barn? She knew what *going to the barn* had

meant when some of her high school classmates, the ones who lived on farms, had said it. Unfortunately, she didn't think that's what Jordan had in mind, though a girl could always hope.

When they reached the barn, he opened the door and gestured for her to precede him into the dim interior. The top half of the door to the first box stall was open, and a bay horse whinnied softly.

Rosemary looked at it. "I don't remember seeing this horse before."

"No, you haven't." Jordan touched her back. "Everybody else got you all those wedding presents, but none of them were from me. This is my wedding present to you, Rosemary."

She drew her breath in sharply. A wedding present. Almost as if he thought of her as a real wife. Or as if he was buying off his conscience?

She reached forward and touched the soft nose. The horse had bright inquiring eyes and a white star in the middle of its forehead.

Jordan stood just behind her, his breath stirring her hair, while she stroked the velvet nose, then rubbed the horse's face, and tangled her hands in the black forelock and in the smooth mane that lay against the side of its neck. "Is this one of the horses you wanted to train? One of the ones we saw in the meadow?"

"No," Jordan said. "I'm starting to work with a few of those since Ken came, but, they're not well enough broken for an inexperienced rider. I got this one just for you. He's a quarter horse, well trained. He's only three years old, but safe and gentle for all of that. The rancher I bought him from guaranteed he'd be perfect for a beginning rider, but just to be sure, I rode him myself."

She wanted to turn and kiss him to show her thanks, but she was afraid that would send him running for the hills again. Instead she leaned forward to rest her forehead against that of the horse. "He's beautiful," she said. "Thank you."

"His name's Jinx." Jordan almost put an arm around her. Sort of laid it against the back of her shoulder. "You have those certificates for a riding school. It's only a few miles away, and they also board horses. I'll ride Jinx over.

155

Then you can pick me up and bring me back. That way, you'll be able to use your own horse for your lessons, and you can go over whenever you feel like it."

Jinx? Hmm. Had Jordan named him? Ah, well. Even if he had it wasn't the horse's fault.

****

Jinx was everything Jordan said he would be—affectionate, gentle, and responsive. Rosemary treasured her riding time. In fact, she went nearly every day while Trevor stayed with Debbie. It was the time that was earmarked for working on her business, but she could work at night.

When she rode, she forgot to obsess about whether or not Jordan would ever come to love her, or how many years this marriage would last, or whether in the end, after all of this, Blair would cruise in with police and/or with lawyers and take Trevor away. When she rode, her mind was on the pleasure of today rather than on the uncertain fears of tomorrow.

Jinx, like a dog, gave unconditional love, so that she never had to worry about what he was thinking of her. She made another decision. She would continue the lessons as long as she enjoyed them and continued to learn. When the gift certificates had been used up, she'd pay for more lessons herself. Just wait until Jordan saw how much progress she'd made, how much control of Jinx she had. Instead of concentrating on staying atop an old and gentle horse, she now enjoyed trotting, cantering and galloping.

One morning she said to Jordan, "I think we can bring Jinx home. I don't need any more lessons."

"Good," he said. "Trevor can come along for the ride."

When they got to the stables, Rosemary put Jinx through his paces, showing Jordan what she had learned. Jordan leaned against the rails of the corral, holding on to Trevor, who perched beside him calling out, "Auntie Wose, Auntie Wose. Hossy. Hossy. Hossy."

When it came time to leave, and Jordan walked toward Jinx, Rosemary said, "I'll ride him home myself. You and Trevor go in the Jeep."

And so they rode on the sparsely traveled country road, Rosemary galloping Jinx on the dirt shoulder,

Jordan driving the Jeep leisurely beside her. Whenever she glanced to the side, he was grinning.

The sweet hot summer wind whipped through her hair. They seemed like a family again, more than they did when they were together in the same room, even the bedroom, ignoring each other.

When they reached home, Rosemary impulsively put her arms around Jordan's neck and kissed his cheek. "Thank you."

He hugged her before he answered, "You're welcome," and let her go.

Life might become good again. The thoughts of Blair and Roscoe and two hundred thousand dollars faded into the background.

****

The phone shrilled soon after breakfast. Rosemary shook off the dim and shadowy tingle of foreboding which unexpected phone calls often brought. From her spot on the floor, she leaned over Trevor and his building blocks to grasp the phone.

Her mother's voice? Crying? Her mother never cried. She was a tower of strength. The dim and shadowy tingle of foreboding exploded into a monster of fear winding its tentacles around Rosemary's heart. "What is it, Mom?" Visions of strokes and heart attacks and car accidents flashed through her mind. Her voice rose. "Is Daddy all right?" A thousand years passed as she waited for the answer.

She heard a sniffle from the other end of the line. "Yes. Daddy's just fine, but, oh, Rosemary, I did the most awful thing."

"Huh." Her mother's idea of awful was a kitchen floor that hadn't been washed for two days. But Daddy was fine and Mom was on the phone. The sky hadn't fallen.

"Oh, Mom. What is it?"

"The pictures. The wedding pictures. I didn't think. Neither of us thought."

A chill wind shook Rosemary as she guessed what was coming.

"Well, I sent them to the paper, and they came out two days ago. They were beautiful. But we should have thought. How could all of us have forgotten? Blair and

Roscoe read the papers too."

"Oh, Mom." She didn't want to know, but she needed to. "What's happening?"

"They're coming out there. They phoned in the middle of the night. Roscoe was in an absolute rage. Swore at me. Said they'd get even."

"Did you talk to Blair?"

"Briefly. I think she's in over her head, but she's afraid of him and can't get away. She couldn't say that because he listened to every word, but I sensed it."

"And?"

"They're on their way. Dad and I are coming on the next flight to Calgary, and we'll rent a car. We don't want you to meet us. Just stay home and protect Trevor."

"You're at home now?"

"No. At the airport. We booked a flight and drove to the airport as soon as Roscoe hung up. We'll be in Calgary shortly. We phoned Len Peterson too. He said he'd round up some men and they'll be right over. Gotta run now. They just called our flight. Be careful. Roscoe bragged about having a gun. He's the most awful man. But they're driving, so we should beat them there by a good bit. Except I'm not sure where they phoned from. Take care."

"You take care too, and thanks." Rosemary mumbled into the phone, but her mother had already hung up.

The wedding pictures. Why had neither of them thought of it? All the secrecy, all the precautions, and then the wedding pictures printed in the newspaper for the whole world to see. Hopefully, Roscoe and Blair were still somewhere in the middle of Saskatchewan, but Rosemary couldn't be sure. They might have phoned her parents from Calgary and even now be closing in on the Sterling ranch.

In a way, it was pathetic, two tough evil people so naïve that in this day and age they considered two hundred thousand dollars to be a fortune. But they were a danger to Trevor for all of that. Rosemary heard tires on the driveway and looked out. Len Peterson. Not Lois. Just Len with a couple other men. The cavalry had arrived.

Rosemary phoned the bungalow. "Debbie, go to the barn. Tell Jordan and Ken that I need them at the house right away. You come too with Dennis. You'll be safer at the house than there by yourselves."

She hung up before Debbie had a chance to question her, and almost immediately she saw Jordan and Ken running from the barn, the two dogs at their heels, Debbie following them more slowly with Dennis in her arms.

Len and the other men got out of the car and spoke briefly to Jordan and Ken, then strolled down the driveway as if on guard duty, which, she supposed, they were.

Jordan hurried into the house. "Anything going on that Len hasn't told me?"

"Probably not," Rosemary said. "He told you that Mom and Dad are on their way?"

Jordan nodded.

"That's about it then. Maybe it's all a bluff, and after two days everybody will go home."

"And maybe it's not."

"Should we call the police?"

"No," Jordan said. "I don't think so. At least not yet. The police might be on Blair's side. The custody hearings aren't complete, and, so far, Blair hasn't done anything illegal. Not that we know about. We'd been sort of basing our case on abandonment, but I guess that's no longer true. I'll phone Sidney and ask him to come over. Legal muscle might be intimidating—at the least buy us a bit more time."

"Mom said that Roscoe bragged about having a gun. Wouldn't that be a reason to call the police? Also a reason to not give Trevor to Blair?"

"Maybe he has a gun and maybe he hasn't. It might have been bravado. Or maybe he carries a registered shotgun or rifle in a case for hunting. And if he doesn't have anything illegal, or even if he has and the police don't find it, calling them might backfire on us."

Debbie ran into the house, still carrying Dennis. Rosemary brought her up to date briefly, trying not to alarm the toddlers, then shoved Trevor at her and told her to take both boys into Trevor's room and amuse them there.

Another car drove in, and parked up the driveway where Len and his friends stood. Three more arrived within the next hour.

"Looks like every rancher for miles around has turned up," Jordan said. "At least that makes Roscoe's gun pretty useless if he has one. He can't possibly shoot that many people."

Privately, Rosemary almost hoped Roscoe would wave the gun around, putting him and Blair on the wrong side of the law.

Sidney Perkins drove up to the house. He closeted himself with Jordan in the living room, where, Rosemary assumed, the two of them were discussing their options. She felt a sense of comfort from the lawyer. At least he'd be able to come up with delaying tactics to keep Blair from waltzing out of the house with Trevor while she and Jordan stood by helplessly. Both Roscoe and Blair would be in awe of the lawyer.

For a time, nothing happened. The ranchers strolled up and down the driveway, gathering in clumps and talking. Ben and Buster wandered among the men, wagging their tails, wanting to be petted.

The next car to appear was the rental with Rosemary's parents in it. Len signaled for it to stop, then waved it on through. Rosemary's parents charged up the steps and into the house, Rosemary's mother still crying, and her husband patting her back. Jordan and the lawyer came into the kitchen to greet them.

"Anything new?" Rosemary asked.

"I think so," her dad said. "There was a car on the highway behind us driving fast and recklessly. It zoomed past the turnoff to your local road, but I suspect it will soon be back."

Jordan smiled tightly. "At least this won't all be for nothing."

Sidney Perkins looked out the kitchen window. "Looks like the next thing to an army preparing for battle out there."

"Right," Jordan told him. "That's the beauty of a rural neighborhood. We all support each other."

Rosemary stood for a moment looking and feeling helpless, but for a moment only. She didn't intend to take part in gun battles, nor even fisticuffs, but after all this was over, the men would be hungry and thirsty.

She turned to her mother. "Mom," she said, "I'll get

160

some bread out of the freezer and you and I can make coffee and sandwiches. Debbie can handle the boys, and hopefully they won't even know anything's going on."

While she worked, she watched out the kitchen window. Shortly another car sped up the driveway, blasting past the waving hands of Len and his friends, who followed on the run.

"Oh, hell." Jordan ran through the kitchen. "He's got even fewer brains than I thought." He left the house.

Roscoe stepped from the car, waving a handgun. "Tell Rosemary to get the kid out here."

"No." Jordan took a step forward. "You deal with me."

"I've got to go out, Mom, and see if I can neutralize all that testosterone out there, before Roscoe gets even more stupid and somebody gets hurt." Rosemary flung down the butter knife and rinsed her hands. "But I'm sure not bringing Trevor. Lock the doors. Oh, yes, and call 911." Now that Roscoe was brandishing an illegal weapon in front of twenty or so witnesses, calling the police was safe.

Rosemary made a show of tripping lightly through the door and down the steps to where she faced Roscoe, with his gun, and Blair. "You can't possibly get by with this nonsense." She tried to affect a nonchalance she didn't feel. "There are more people here than you can possibly shoot and if you try all you'll accomplish is life in prison for both of you." She turned to Blair. "How could you have let him talk you into something this stupid?"

"Trevor's my baby," Blair mumbled. "I have a right to him."

"Not after this fiasco, you don't. Now why don't you convince Roscoe to put that gun away and leave?"

Blair gave Roscoe an uncertain look. "Maybe we shouldn't."

"Shut your mouth and hold this." He handed her the gun. "Keep it pointed at these nice folks, and if they try anything funny, don't be afraid to use it. I'm getting the kid myself, and this pretty lady is going with me to show me where he is."

He grabbed Rosemary and twisted one arm behind her back, jerking it up until she had to bite her lip to keep from screaming with pain. There was no way she'd give

161

him the satisfaction. Roscoe's breath smelled of whisky. His florid face was far too close to hers, and his beer-belly pressed against her thigh.

Rosemary closed her eyes to block him out. Dear God, how long would this nightmare go on? She opened her eyes. She needed all her wits about her, needed to see what went on around her, no matter how repulsive Roscoe was.

Jordan took another step forward. "Let her go. You need a hostage, take me."

"Very noble of you." Roscoe sneered at him. "But I prefer the pretty lady." Roscoe jerked Rosemary's arm up again. She could no longer stifle a sound of pain.

Everything happened at once.

Two furry yellow bodies flashed out of the crowd. Ben and Buster. Before Rosemary took the whole thing in, Ben was at Roscoe's throat. Roscoe's grip on Rosemary loosened.

"Shoot them," Roscoe yelled at Blair. "Shoot the dogs." But while Blair fumbled with the gun, Buster threw all his hundred pounds at her, knocking her flat.

Jordan grabbed the revolver, while several men wrestled Roscoe to the ground.

Rosemary watched, stunned, and rubbed her aching arm.

She remembered the first day she'd met the dogs. Jordan had said then, *Once they know you, they'll defend you with their lives.*

The sound of sirens filled the air.

****

Rosemary watched as Roscoe and Blair were put into a police car, Blair sobbing that it hadn't been her idea and that she wanted counseling to put her life together. Rosemary resolved that, after the dust settled, she'd talk to some of the social workers she'd spent so much time with. They'd surely know the right channels to get Blair the help she needed.

The vigilantes enjoyed the coffee and sandwiches and drove back to their ranches.

Sidney Perkins volunteered the information that the most recent report from the private investigator would probably have scuttled Blair's chances anyway.

Apparently Roscoe had taken to hanging around daycare centers.

There was no further risk that Trevor might be given to his mother.

After dinner, Rosemary put Trevor to bed, and a few hours later settled her parents into the guest room. Jordan and Rosemary sat in the family room pretending to watch television.

Rosemary didn't know what Jordan was thinking, but she was thinking of how sterile that wide bed seemed with the two of them in it, though they were only a foot apart. How long could she endure this farce? She supposed the bright spot was that she now knew for sure that she wasn't pregnant. Somehow, even that was faintly depressing. She tried to turn her attention back onto the sitcom that filled the television screen.

"I think I'll turn in." Jordan stretched and yawned. "It's been a long day. At some point we'll have to talk to Sidney about our marriage, but I guess it can wait until after your parents leave."

Rosemary suddenly snapped to attention, but Jordan had already left the room. She turned off the television and began to pace, head bowed, her left hand pressed above her upper lip. The only sound was the soft padding of her sock feet against the floor. Her mind raced around and around, like a gerbil on a treadmill. Did she give up? Did she give in? Did she fight for her place on the ranch, with Trevor?

This was going nowhere. She'd have visitation rights with Trevor, of course. Jordan had promised that. What about Ken and Debbie and Dennis? Did she get visitation rights with them? Or did she become a pleasant but distant figure in their memories? And Ben and Buster? Probably an exaggeration to say they'd saved her life, but they'd sure reduced the danger in a hurry.

What about Jinx? Jinx was hers, given to her, a wedding present from her husband. Did she have visitation rights with him too, or did Jordan expect her to take him to her apartment in Winnipeg or a new apartment in Calgary? Huh!

Jinx. Tears misted her eyes as she thought of him. Unconditional love—Jinx's feelings toward her, and hers toward him. She remembered her rides on Jinx. The times when the problems of everyday life disappeared.

That's what she needed right now.

A long ride on Jinx.

Why not? It might be nearly midnight, but the bad guys were safely tucked away in police lock-up. The ranch held no risks. Rosemary wasn't afraid of bears or coyotes or things that went bump in the night. She stalked to the back door and shoved her boots on, then took off for the barn.

Jinx nickered a welcome as she opened the barn door. She pressed her forehead against his and clasped the sides of his head in her hands, letting his comfort flow into her. "Come on, boy. We're going for a ride, you and I." Their last ride? She hoped not. It was a matter of moments to throw on his saddle and bridle and lead him from the barn.

She chose the path that led beside the creek, the creek she loved, along with everything else on this ranch. When she reached the spot where the cowslips bloomed and a large rock perfect for sitting was near the bank, she stopped Jinx, dismounted, and ground-tied him. Not that he would ever stray from her. He wasn't like human males. She sat on the rock, her head in her hands.

What came next?

Obviously, Jordan expected her to disappear as soon as doing so wouldn't cause an unpleasant scene with her parents. Oh, yes. The nice family visit, then the end. Sort of like that famous last meal for a condemned man. Jordan said they'd talk about the marriage, but somehow she didn't think he was talking about salvaging it. She gazed at the rippling light where the moon danced on the water.

In spite of herself, the tears came. Jinx rubbed his velvet nose against the back of her head. She automatically reached back and scratched his face.

She scrambled up from the rock and wrapped her arms around Jinx's neck and cried into the blackness of his mane. Jinx probably thought she was crazy, but he loved her anyway, as she loved him, and Trevor, and Ben and Buster, and the house, and the ranch, and even, God help her, Jordan Sterling.

She'd invested in Trevor for his whole life, and she'd invested several months in Jordan. Now, she was supposed to leave quietly, with visiting rights, pre-scheduled undoubtedly, if she wanted them.

Well, she had news for Jordan Sterling. She'd suffered the suspicious looks of tradespeople because of him. In spite of that, she'd made a lot of friends in this community, friends for both herself and Trevor, and she'd been the means of Jordan renewing old friendships.

And now, he expected her to walk away from all of it. *I don't think so.*

No, she would not. Would not give up this easily.

We'll talk about the marriage, will we? So now he hasn't any more worries about Trevor, he can just toss me aside like a worn-out tire. Well, don't do me any favors. Maybe I have something to say about what happens next.

Maybe he didn't love her the way she loved him, but he didn't find her repulsive either. She remembered the scene on the piano bench, where they'd kissed until she'd pushed him away. She remembered the picnic in the mountain meadow when they'd flirted and kissed. She remembered his behavior on their wedding day, a masterful performance for a man who'd never been on a stage in his life. Finally, she remembered his telling her that he didn't love her. She had told him that too. Maybe, just maybe, they'd both been lying.

She made up her mind. She was through with telling lies, through with accepting them, through with letting stubbornness and pride rule her life.

It was time she asserted herself and demanded what was hers.

Just as she placed her left foot in the stirrup, she heard a noise of someone or something approaching. She quickly finished mounting.

"What the hell do you think you're doing out here?" Jordan? And the two dogs.

She drew herself up in the saddle, sitting so erect that she felt six feet tall. "Maybe I should ask you the same thing?" She infused her voice with all the haughtiness she could muster.

"I was worried. I heard you go out, and thought you were just getting a breath of air. But you didn't come back. Eventually I got concerned. Jinx was missing from the barn."

"I thought you wanted me to disappear and never come back." She gentled her voice a notch and continued. "How'd you find me?"

"The dogs followed the trail. They're very useful in case you haven't noticed."

"I've noticed."

"Why did you come out here like this?"

"I wanted to think more about what you said. About discussing our marriage as soon as my parents leave."

"Yes?"

"Yes. And I'd like to share some of my thoughts with you right now."

"Fine." Jordan grasped Jinx's reins and began to lead him back down the path, toward home. "Share away."

"I intend to share Trevor, and not on a visitation basis either. I've known Trevor a lot longer than you have, and he wouldn't be here if it weren't for me." She sat with both hands grasping the saddle horn. "I've taken care of your house and I intend to go on doing that."

Jordan held up one hand as if to stop her, but she was on a roll and wasn't about to stop.

"I'm not finished," she said to his back. "I'm going to share your ranch too, and never mind bringing up those papers I signed with your lawyer. It's the house and the community I want. Just in case you haven't noticed, I've made a lot of friends here and I'm going to keep them. And Jinx. What about Jinx? Am I supposed to find an apartment that takes horses? I'm not interested in the financial part of the ranch and I'm not interested in your damned oil wells. Furthermore, Jordan Sterling, I love you, and I'm going to keep you too. You've shown a reasonable interest in my body more than once, and I think we'll do just fine even if you can't love me the way I love you—"

"Whoa. Whoa there." He shouted the words. Jinx halted so suddenly that Rosemary rocked forward in the saddle. "Easy, boy," Jordan said to the horse. "I didn't mean you."

He turned to face Rosemary. "Rosemary, be quiet for a minute. Of course, I love you. I think I've loved you ever

166

since I saw you standing in a blizzard in those foolish shorts."

"Maybe you should have shared that with me."

They stood under the yard light, and Rosemary saw Jordan close his eyes. "I wanted to, but I couldn't." His face looked tired and drawn. "You were so young and vital and beautiful. How could I burden you with the knowledge that I loved you? It wouldn't have been fair."

"Oh, Jordan. I thought I was only a nanny to you. And that when you were attracted to me, it was just lust."

When they reached the barn door, Jordan slung the reins back over Jinx's neck. "All right." Jordan leaned against the horse and looked up at Rosemary. "Among all these things you want to share, is my bed one of them? That is, really share it? Not just coexist in it?"

She smiled at him. Finally smiled widely, a great weight lifting from her heart and soul. "Of course." She tumbled off Jinx and into Jordan's arms. "I want to share your bed the way I shared it on our wedding night. Always."

He kissed her on the nose. "Then welcome home, Rosemary."

A word about the author...

Wilma Fasano grew up in Western Alberta, lived and worked for many years in Northern Manitoba, and now makes her home in Nova Scotia with her husband Jim. The Fasano's enjoy travel, their winter home in Florida, and their three beautiful grandchildren.

Books published (all by Avalon Books): Weekend Romance; Love Song; The Love Game; and Dolphin Song

Excerpt from a review of Dolphin Song: The author's writing style is quick and spare, there is no purple prose here. Those who are looking for a quick read with a fun setting and a likable couple will enjoy this story. Linda Hurst

Printed in the United States
118271LV00001B/1-24/A

9 781601 541055